GEORGE DOUGLAS

ODD WOMAN OUT

Complete and Unabridged

LINFORD
Leicester

First published in Great Britain by
Robert Hale Limited
London

First Linford Edition
published 2006
by arrangement with
Robert Hale Limited
London

British Library CIP Data

Douglas, George
Odd woman out.—Large print ed.—
Linford mystery library
1. Murder—Investigation—Fiction
2. Detective and mystery stories
3. Large type books
I. Title
823.9′14 [F]

ISBN 1–84617–371–X

Published by
F. A. Thorpe (Publishing)
Anstey, Leicestershire

Set by Words & Graphics Ltd.
Anstey, Leicestershire
Printed and bound in Great Britain by
T. J. International Ltd., Padstow, Cornwall

This book is printed on acid-free paper

1

On a fine September morning, P.C. Richard Garrett of the Deniston Police cruised gently on motor-cycle patrol along the city's Northway Ring Road. At seven-fifteen a.m. things were always quiet, and here, on the city boundary, there were still fields and woods. Garrett, a country-bred lad, used his eyes appreciatively.

He came quietly to a halt opposite a gateway, the better to watch a kestrel hovering over a piece of wheat stubble. But his feet were no sooner on the ground than his call signal stuttered urgently from his radio.

Garrett answered it smartly. He gave his position. The voice from Headquarters spoke impersonally.

'Go to Granville Road, Ashwood. Investigate report of a woman's body found in a garden there. Mr. Reginald Kaye, of Twenty-six Granville Road, will meet you at that address.'

Garrett acknowledged the order, and, a quarter of a mile farther on, swung away from the Ring Road towards Ashwood. He knew his way about the suburb, for it lay on the northern perimeter of his normal beat.

Ashwood Road, on which he was travelling now, ran through the centre of the residential area. Granville Road lay at the far end, separated from the extensive Ash Wood, which had named the district, by a narrow unpaved path known as Gypsy Lane.

Number Twenty-six was the last house on the left of Granville Road. Garrett dismounted at the double gates, both of which were open, and left his machine on the tarmacadamed drive which led to the garage and the house.

The man who answered the door was in his early forties, below average height but thickset, with wide shoulders and powerful legs. He was dark-haired, dark-eyed, heavily browed. Even in a state of early morning dishevelment and needing a shave, he carried about him the air of a professional man, and a successful one at that.

'Mr. Reginald Kaye?'

'Yes, yes. Come in.' Kaye turned and led the way to a french-windowed lounge. 'You must excuse me not being dressed yet. I just haven't had time. I mean, I thought I ought to be available when you arrived.' He jerked a thumb. 'Out there. In the next-door garden. You can't see her from here.'

Above them a muted tumult arose, children's voices in the full flush of early-morning energy. Kaye smiled briefly.

'My two young sons. Their mother and — well, we have a guest — they are keeping the boys out of the way.'

'Do I understand it was you who found the dead person, sir?'

'Yes. I took a stroll up my own garden, as I often do on a fine morning while I wait for the kettle to boil, you know. Early tea, and all that. I saw her lying there.'

'You'll have told your next-door neighbours, I take it?'

'I haven't. They are an elderly couple and the woman has a dicky heart. They won't be up for at least an hour yet, anyway. Well, come on, let's get it over. I'll show you the way. Through my garden, since you won't want us trampling about the Rennisons' place any more than we can help, I suppose?'

Garrett said, 'You have the right idea, sir,' and followed the dressing-gowned figure, with a deliberate tensing of his stomach muscles, an exercise he had always found helpful on approaching any sort of unpleasantness in the line of duty. Kaye stood back when they reached a low wall, and after a careful survey of the ground ahead, Garret jumped over to bend briefly beside the woman who lay in a patch of potatoes. There was no doubt that she was dead. He returned to the wall.

'Do you know who she is, sir?'

'A Miss Adkin. She lives — lived — at Number Eight up yonder.' His head jerked to the left. 'By herself, I believe.'

'Right.' Garret rejoined him. 'I'll just go and put in a preliminary report, sir, and it'll be my job to stand by here until the C.I.D. people arrive.'

The orders he expected followed his report, and he went back towards the house, unbuttoning his tunic pocket to reach his notebook. As he was passing the kitchen door it opened and a woman stood there, leaning negligently against the door jamb.

She was tall, beautifully made, a Norse goddess with her shining blonde hair, her large blue eyes and clear, faintly-rosy complexion. But a second look revealed the lines on her forehead, her small, ill-tempered mouth, her age-scored neck. Garrett took that second look after he had noted, lingeringly, the full curves of her body, generously emphasized by the thin, low-necked house-coat belted tightly to her. Under it she wore a transparent nylon nightie, with pompommed slippers on her bare feet.

'Hullo!' she said in a voice which came out warm and slightly husky. 'Isn't this a terrible business? It is to us, at any rate. You're probably used to that sort of thing. I've just made coffee. You'll join us, won't you?'

She stepped aside invitingly, smiling

into his eyes. Garrett grinned back at her easily. He'd got over the initial jolt of her appearance, he saw she must be in her middle thirties at least and that her teeth were not her own. To a young chap of twenty-three she was just another married woman, obviously making the most of what wouldn't last much longer, anyhow.

'Sorry,' he said, 'but the brass may be here any minute, and if they caught me being sociable they'd throw the book. I'll just step in and take a few names down, though. I've a report to make.'

The kitchen was spacious, equipped with all the appliances Garrett's mother often wished for but couldn't afford. The policeman glanced inquiringly at a big, red-haired man in trousers and a collarless shirt who was leaning against the sink.

Mrs. Kaye said, 'Oh, this is Mr. Pettifer. He's staying here.'

Pettifer, a little uneasy, it seemed, under Garrett's professionally calculating eye, heaved himself upright and landed a playful smack on Mrs. Kaye's buttock as she moved past him to the stove.

'That's right, pet.' He frowned as Garrett opened his notebook. 'Listen, Jack. I don't know nothing about this, see? First I hear of it, Reg wakes me up and tells me. I've never even met that dame out yonder.'

'It's not my job to take statements, sir. The C.I.D. will do that. But I have to get some details down. For instance, your husband's work, Mrs. Kaye?'

'He's an accountant, at Sims and Forrester, Bellman Street.'

And a very nice job that must be, Garrett thought a few minutes later as he stood leaning against the wall at the end of the garden, his back to the potato patch on the far side of it. Fine detached house in a good district, all modern furnishings and frills, a still-handsome wife. There was just one item which didn't seem to fit. The man Pettifer. Not the sort of guest you'd expect to meet in such a typical suburban family.

2

Detective Chief Inspector William Hallam was tall, lean and lantern-jawed. Light brown hair topped a broad forehead and a penetrating pair of grey eyes. There was an air of impatiently-controlled energy about him; as he sat in the deep armchair which Reginald Kaye had insisted he should use his left foot beat lightly on the carpet, the fingers of his right hand played intermittent scales on his thigh.

He looked up at Kaye, now dressed in a dark, well-cut business suit, white shirt, claret-red tie and highly polished shoes.

'Just let me check I have your story correctly, sir. You got up at your usual time this morning and while waiting for the kettle to boil you strolled down the garden. A habit of yours?'

'On a nice day, yes, Chief Inspector. I enjoy a breath of fresh morning air.'

'Exactly. Now, you heard nothing unusual during the night? Nobody moving about outside, no front gates opening or closing?'

'Not a thing. I'm a sound sleeper, Chief Inspector.'

'I take it you and Mrs. Kaye use the front bedroom, usually the biggest one in a house of this type?'

'Yes.' Kaye's glance flickered, then steadied on Hallam's face again. 'That is, in normal circumstances. Recently, however, my wife has been unwell and we thought it better if I used the small room over the front porch. Originally it was my — let us say den, as it is far too modest to be called a study. We have had a camp bed put up there.'

'And your guest, Mr. Pettifer, also heard nothing?'

'So he tells me.'

'Right, sir.' Hallam rose. 'I won't keep you any longer. Thanks for a very lucid narrative of events.'

Kaye smiled thinly. 'Lucidity is a basic factor of accountancy, Chief Inspector.'

He turned to open the door and stepped aside to let Hallam precede him. As they went along the hall to the front door, Kaye cleared his throat.

'I take it you will want to see my wife and Mr. Pettifer, Chief Inspector, though they can tell you even less than I?'

'Yes, just for the record, sir. Later on, though. I'll wait until the boys have gone to school.'

'That's extremely thoughtful of you. Naturally, the less Patrick and Gordon know of this, the better. Another thing occurs to me. You'll need the use of a telephone. So I'll leave this front door on the latch. Come right in and help yourself anytime you wish.'

Hallam thanked him, bade him good morning.

A lean, rangy man with the air of a terrier which has heard the word 'rats' was coming through the drive gates. Detective Sergeant George Spratt was, inevitably, known to one and all as 'Jack.'

'Just coming to contact you, sir,' he said. 'Dr. Ransome's arrived. I thought you'd like a word with him.'

Hallam nodded. 'Any luck?'

'Not a scrap.' They had moved to the drive of the semi-detached house next door. 'These iron gates were both shut — I've fastened them back so the scientists can have a closer look presently — and there's nothing to be seen all the way up the garden. You go ahead, sir, and you'll see what I mean.'

'Have you roused these Rennisons?'

'I managed to get the old man moving by leaning on the front door bell for quite a time. He must be in his eighties, but he's all there still. Said he knew nothing about it, hadn't heard nor seen a thing. He's going to get his wife up, and they'll keep out of the way till we want them.'

'Good.' Hallam walked forward. The garden beyond the house was as long as that of Kaye's, but only half the width. There was a narrow shrubbery at the end of the lawn, by-passed by the two flagged paths, and a vegetable garden beyond it. The paths here were of rough clinker and Hallam's shoes grated loudly as he approached the man who was kneeling on a folded tarpaulin, provided by Spratt as part of the murder kit he maintained in the boot of the police car.

'Morning, Doctor. Sorry to drag you out so early.'

Dr. Ransome was small-boned, neat and dapper. His fingers moved with a precise swiftness as he replaced his instruments in his case.

'Can't be helped.' He got to his feet and nodded to Police Constable Garrett who had been standing by. 'Right, lad. You can help the sergeant to cover her with this tarp.' He turned to Hallam. 'Manual strangulation, without any question, but I doubt if you'll get much from the finger imprints. She also struck the back of her head on some hard surface, or was struck there. No bleeding, though. Which came first, the blow or the strangling? I'll need to have her on the table to answer that. And she's been dead between four and eight hours.'

Hallam thanked him, Ransome said, 'Good morning, all,' and went back to his car. Hallam looked at his sergeant.

'So we have a middle-aged woman, quite a good looker in her time, dressed in black cord slacks and a black leather jacket, lying in a bed of potatoes after having been strangled and bashed, or the other way round, maybe.'

'But not killed here,' Spratt said. 'No evidence of a struggle.' He gestured, questioningly, at the beech hedge across the top of the garden. There was a narrow wicket gate at one corner of it.

'Yes,' Hallam agreed. 'Worth a look. You go to Kaye's, Sergeant, and ring for the usual gang. The front door's open, the phone's just inside on a window ledge. No need to bother the household, I've arranged all that with Kaye. Meanwhile, Garrett and I'll nose around a bit.'

Garrett followed the Chief Inspector past the potatoes, where the cinder path ended at a piece of bare, undug ground.

'Watch where you put your feet,' Hallam warned. 'Ground's well-trodden and dry as a bone, but there might be something to find. We'll keep clear of a direct line between the body and the gate.

'Home-made contraption,' he commented as Garrett unlatched the gate and swung it back on its strip-leather hinges. They passed through to Gypsy Lane, a narrow dusty path which ran behind the houses from Ashwood Road at their upper end. Beyond the houses it became a mere track over Granville Common. On the other side of the lane Ash Wood thrust out a broad arm, bordered by a rough post-and-wire fence which sagged throughout its length.

'Footprints, lots of 'em, pram and bicycle tracks and assorted litter galore,' Hallam muttered as he looked up and down the lane. 'Well, it'll all have to be gone over, in case she was brought this way. What's the building backing into the wood up yonder?'

'It's a wooden bungalow, sir. Man named Tanner lives there with his widowed sister. He has a bit of a small-holding and does jobbing gardening on the side. I had to call on him some weeks ago. A traffic accident on the main road, and he was a witness. Then, beyond the wood, before you get to Ashwood Road, there's another house, sir. The wood hides it from here. It's part of a small riding school.'

'Right. You keep an eye on this lane, try to stop anybody using it until we can start a search. Report to me before you go back on patrol.'

'Yes, sir.' Garrett hesitated, and then, 'This Miss Adkin, sir. I spoke to her about a fortnight since. She was walking up this lane about one in the morning.'

'Go on.'

'I was on night patrol. I'd pulled up on the roadside just past the top of Gypsy Lane here. That's the limit of my patrol, sir. I'd switched off the engine and I was just — well, just sitting there, sir.'

'Catching a quiet smoke.' Hallam grinned. 'Yes, I know. Used to do that sort of thing myself.'

'Well, sir, this lady came out of the mouth of the lane, dressed like she is now. When she saw me she stopped and I got the impression she'd have dodged back out of sight, only she knew I'd spotted her. So she came up to me and passed some remark on the weather and then said, 'I expect you're wondering what I'm doing out at this time of night. As a matter of fact, I'm interested in ornithology — bird watching, you know. I'm doing some private research on the local owl population, there are still plenty around here.' I said I'd just been listening to a couple calling to each other and she said, 'Yes, there they go again. What would an English night be without the call of the Barn Owl?' Then she said she'd better be getting home and turned down Granville Road, sir.'

'And the point of all the detail, Garrett, apart from the fact that she may have made a habit of night-strolling?'

'They were Tawny Owls that were calling, sir. As anybody should have known, especially a bird watcher.'

'Quite,' Hallam returned. To him an owl was an owl, just that. 'I'll bear in mind what you've told me. Now you watch this lane, and don't go looking for clues to pass the time. That's a specialist's job.'

He walked back to the gate. Sergeant Spratt was there, marshalling the half-dozen official cars which, apparently, had all arrived at once.

'I'll leave you to set this gang to work, Jack,' Hallam said. 'Then we'll see if the Rennisons are ready to answer a few questions.' He looked at his watch. 'Nine-fifteen. The Super'll be at the office by now. I'll ring him from next door and give him the outline.'

Hallam walked along the Kayes' drive. The open doors of the empty garage showed that Kaye had already left for business. Hallam turned the handle of the front door and stepped into the hall, almost treading on the toes of a buxom blonde in a flowered print dress and sandals who stood there, the telephone at one ear, an unlighted cigarette in her free hand.

She smiled at Hallam and put everything she had into the smile. Then she made a small, self-excusing grimace at the telephone, shrugging her heavy shoulders, and dropping the cigarette.

'Sorry about this. Shan't be a moment.' She put her hand on Hallam's shoulder as he bent to pick up the cigarette. 'Thanks. Be a darling and hold it for me.'

Hallam glanced past her. The kitchen door at the end of the hall was open, and he had the distinct impression a man had been standing there as he had entered, a man who had dodged back when he saw who had come in.

'Yes,' Mrs. Kaye was saying, 'I'm sorry but I can't see you this morning. Something's happened here and we're all at sixes and sevens . . . No, I'll ring you again later and fix something up. I must go now because a most gorgeous policeman is here, wanting to talk to me.'

She banged the handset on to its studs and took the cigarette from Hallam's fingers. He found a box of matches and struck one for her. She held his hand with both of hers as she drew the flame towards the cigarette.

'You do want to talk to me, don't you?' she asked.

'Yes. You're Mrs. Kaye, of course. But I would like to use the telephone first, if I may.'

'Be my guest, and welcome. Just give me a call when you're ready for me — Inspector, is it?'

'Detective Chief Inspector Hallam, madam.'

'Oh, I couldn't possibly say all that. I'll just call you 'Chief.' I'll be in the kitchen.'

She went along the hall, closing the kitchen door behind her. Hallam heard a man's voice there as he dialled his Superintendent, made his brief report and was told to 'carry on as usual, Bill.'

He walked to the kitchen door and tapped on it. Mrs. Kaye appeared at once.

'Let's go into the lounge,' she suggested with her warm smile turned full on. When she had settled Hallam in the deep chair he had used before, she perched on the broad arm of another one, crossing her legs and showing him plenty of them.

'Now, Chief,' she invited. 'Let's go.'

'Did you hear anyone moving about outside during last night, Mrs. Kaye?'

'No, I'm sure I didn't, Chief. And my name's Stella. Don't let's be formal.'

'No sound of the Rennisons' gates opening or closing?'

She shook her blonde head decisively.

'Your husband told me he went to bed at about a quarter past eleven. I take it you retired at the same time?'

'Well, actually, no. When we'd got rid of him, Sidney — that's Mr. Pettifer — and I sat on here talking for a while.'

‘Until when?’

‘Oh, it would be — well, I should say about two o’clock when we broke it up.’ She had begun to speak hesitatingly, looking away from him, then suddenly words came with a rush.

‘You said something about people prowling around outside. Well, Sidney Pettifer did hear footsteps, or thought he did, several nights ago. Round at the back here. His room overlooks the lawn, you see. He got up and looked out of the window, but it was dark and he couldn’t see anything. He told us about it next morning. Would you like a word with him?’

‘Yes, perhaps I’d better.’

‘I’ll fetch him.’ Hallam heard what seemed to be a brief altercation in the kitchen and then the big red-haired man he had glimpsed came into the lounge. He gave the impression Mrs. Kaye had had to push him all the way there.

‘How do,’ he said glumly. ‘What’s all this about me hearing people in the garden? I never said I did, I only said I thought as I did. Coulda bin dreaming, or mebbe I had one over the odds that night. 'Sides, it weren't last night, anyway.'

'What night was it, sir?'

'Let's see. Today's Tuesday, musta bin last Friday or Sat'day. Ask Stella here. She seems to know more about it nor I do.'

'But, Sid, you know you said — '

Hallam broke in quickly. 'If you're not definite, sir, it's probably of no consequence. Now, Mrs. Kaye tells me you and she were sitting here last night until about two o'clock — '

'And what if we was? That's no crime, is it?'

Mrs. Kaye put a hand on his arm and frowned at him as Hallam's fingers began to tap on his knee.

'Mr. Pettifer, I'm investigating a homicide. It's important to discover, if I can, exactly when the victim met her death. It could have been in the very early hours of this morning. You and Mrs. Kaye were up until two. It's possible you heard something which could be of help.'

'Well, I didn't,' Pettifer said sulkily. 'Never saw or heard nothing. So that's it.'

Hallam got up. 'Thank you both. I hope I shan't have to trouble you again. By the way, Mr. Pettifer, I understand you're a guest here. May I have your permanent address?'

Pettifer scowled. 'I dunno what for. But it's Sixty-three Dean Street. That's Deniston 2, in case you don't know.'

'Right. Thank you again.' Hallam let himself out. Neither Stella Kaye nor Pettifer seemed anxious to do the normal courtesies.

Sergeant Spratt was waiting for him. 'Nothing doing yet, sir. Neither in the garden nor in the lane nor the wood. I've sent Garrett to the Tanners' bungalow since he already knows the people there. And I told him to call at that riding school, too. Ambulance has just left. I searched the body but only found this.' He held up a latchkey.

'Good. Then I think you and I had better see the Rennisons next.' He frowned, looking back at the house he had just left. 'Something odd there, you know. It doesn't fit. Why should a man, a roughish type by the look and sound of him, be a guest in a house like that? And what sort of husband would go to bed in a spare room while his wife and the said guest sat up talking until the small hours? Sixty-three Dean Street. Just jot that down in your notebook, Jack.'

3

Police Constable Garrett walked carefully up Gypsy Lane, moving along the grass verge. The wooden bungalow to which he was bound carried a sign, 'Wood Lea,' on its freshly-painted gate. He went up the short path to the front door between neat, well-kept borders. The bungalow was set in a clearing some sixty yards wide, and Garrett knew there was more than an acre of ground at the back.

Garrett's knock brought a tall, handsome woman of late middle age to the door. She recognized him with a pleasant smile.

'Are you wanting to see my brother again?'

'Probably both of you, Mrs. Mason. I've been sent to make some inquiries — look, if Mr. Tanner's around, maybe I could tell you both at once?'

'Come you into the kitchen then, and I'll find James. He's out at the back somewhere.'

Garrett followed her along a central passage and went through the door she indicated. It was a neat, workmanlike kitchen, with an old-fashioned range and a vast sink with a wooden draining-board, well scrubbed.

Boots rasped on a metal scraper outside the back door and James Tanner followed his sister in. He was a strongly-built man in his late fifties, with a weathered complexion and eyes of a startlingly light blue. He nodded at Garrett.

'What's to do now then, young man?'

'Something very bad, I'm afraid, Mr. Tanner. You'll know Miss Adkin?'

'Ay, I know that bitch, to me sorrow.' The words, despite their connotation, were spoken slowly and without viciousness, but his sister drew her breath in sharply.

'Now, James, that's no way to talk!'

'It's honest talk, however, Jean, lass. She's no friend to me, and well you know it. What about her, anyway?'

'She's dead, Mr. Tanner. She's been killed. She was found in Rennison's garden this morning.'

Mrs. Mason gave a choked cry — 'Oh, no!' — and Tanner's mouth dropped open as he stared at the policeman.

'Nay, lad!' He managed it after a deep gulp. 'Dead, you say? Killed? I can't believe it.'

'It's true, though.' Garrett let his words hang in a long silence. Mrs. Mason had sunk into the chair by the table and she sat there, staring at the floor. Tanner scowled, scratched his head, fumbled a pipe from a side pocket and pushed it back again. Garrett gave them time to rein in their galloping thoughts.

'Yes,' he said. 'It's a bad job. She was killed some time during last night. She could have been in or around Gypsy Lane. That's why I'm here, to find out if either of you saw or heard anything.'

'Not me,' Tanner muttered. 'I was in bed at half-nine last night. I get up early and I was tired. Dropped off at once. Never woke.'

'Mrs. Mason?'

The woman's head came up and her eyes were distant in an effort of recollection.

'I stayed up to watch a television programme till eleven. It would be near on half-past when I got to bed. I'm not one who goes off to sleep quickly, it usually takes me an hour or more. I was just sort of drifting off when I remembered a fowl which James had killed for me yesterday morning and hung on a nail in the side porch. Well, I'd forgotten to bring it in, and there's still a fox or two in Ash Wood. So I put on my dressing-gown and came through the house. And when I was lifting the fowl down I heard somebody walking down the lane. It was too dark to see anything, but I'd swear it was a woman's walk. Short, light steps, you know.'

Garrett had his notebook out. 'And that would be — when, Mrs. Mason?'

'Quarter past one. I looked at my bedside clock when I got back to my room.'

'Thanks. That could be helpful.' He put the notebook away. 'What was the trouble between you and Miss Adkin, then, Mr. Tanner?'

Tanner scratched his head again. 'It

sounds daft now, but it were all over her cat. Her garden backs on Gypsy Lane, you see, a bit further up nor what we are. Well, this cat got the habit, like, of coming into our place for its morning stroll, and pawing in me seed beds to do its business. What's more, it killed a couple of me chicks some time back. So I saw Miss Adkin about it and all she'd say was, well, that's a cat's nature and you can't change it. So I told her next time her damn Tiddles came round my place, he'd get my boot in his bottom. 'Course, I didn't really mean it.'

'But she didn't like it?'

'She was hopping mad. She was going to report me to everything from the R.S.P.C.A. to flippin' Interpol. I told her to go ahead and good luck to her. 'Course nothing came of that and she did keep old Tiddles away from here. But she went around telling folks I was no use as a jobbing gardener, overcharged and wasted time on the job. Didn't do me any harm, like, that sort of talk, for folks know me around here, but I didn't like it and you can see why I said what I did about her.'

'James wouldn't have — I mean, you mustn't think — anyway, he was asleep at the time,' his sister said confusedly and Garrett, putting on his crash helmet, gave her a half-wink.

'You could swear to that last statement in Court, Mrs. Mason?'

'Of course. That is . . . ' Her words trailed off. Tanner reached out and touched her shoulder, grinning at Garrett.

'Never knows when her leg's being pulled, doesn't this one,' he said.

Garrett continued up Gypsy Lane. Chief Inspector Hallam would be interested to know Miss Adkin was alive at one-fifteen, and proceeding towards the spot where her body was found — if it had been Miss Adkin whom Mrs. Mason had heard.

He stopped at a larger bungalow set at the edge of a field just above the wood. A board announced 'Ashwood House Riding School. Charles Crane, Prop.' in black lettering. Side gates of ironwork led into a concreted yard surrounded by ranges of stabling and a big barn, and beyond these, in a field, Garrett could see several ponies and one handsome weight-carrying hunter.

He walked into the yard. In one of the stables a horse whinnied urgently, demanding its feed, and a young man came out of the barn, carrying a corn-filled sieve. He looked up, saw Garrett and dodged back at once into the barn. Promptly, Garrett followed him.

There was a range of corn bins along one side of the barn with a big window above. The young man was bending over one of the bins; he was delving so deeply into it that he seemed to be about to stand on his head. Garrett walked across to him and spoke quietly.

'Mr. Crane?'

'No.' The reply was muffled. 'He's in the house. Knock at the back door.'

'Thanks.' Garrett made no move away from the bin. He stood there whistling softly to himself. A half-minute ticked slowly away before the arched body straightened and a pair of light-grey eyes, aggressively challenging, stared into his.

'You want me to show you the way, or something?'

‘No. No, it’s okay.’ Garrett spoke almost absently, studying the other man. He was sparsely built, with coal-black hair and eyebrows. A narrow face, based on a chin firmly protuberant, was, at the moment, duskily-red with stooping. Items of a recent radio message began to tick themselves off in the policeman’s brain.

‘You working here, then?’ Garrett was still casual. He took a step forward and glanced into the bin.

‘Yeah. I like horses. Been with ’em all me life. You know, racing stables and that.’

Garrett nodded and turned away. ‘I’ll go and find the boss, then,’ he said and crossed the barn into the morning sunshine. He found a door, partly open. His knock brought a ‘Come right in!’ from somewhere and he walked along a passage into a kitchen where a man sat at a small table, finishing his breakfast.

‘Oh! Good morning!’ The man rose, dropping the paper he had been reading on to the floor as Garrett appeared, removing his helmet. ‘Police, is it? Dear me! What can I do for you?’

'Mr. Crane?'

'Yes. Charles Crane.' The riding-school proprietor was tall, darkly handsome with a natural wave to well-barbered hair, a lean face and a supple, gracefully-balanced body. He wore a canary-coloured polo jumper, immaculately clean tailored riding-breeches and grey stockings above a pair of carpet slippers.

'I'm here to make some inquiries, sir.'

'Indeed?' Crane stooped suddenly to pick up his paper. He folded it carefully and laid it on the table, looking down at it as if his eye had caught a paragraph of intense interest.

'Inquiries?' he repeated.

'Yes, sir. D'you happen to know a Miss Adkin, of Granville Road?'

Crane released a slow breath. 'I'm afraid I don't. Not by name, anyway. We've not been here long — a couple of years — and I'm too busy a man to know many of my neighbours.'

'Middle-aged lady, sir. Tall, well made. Hair going grey.'

'No. Sorry. What's the trouble, then?'

'She was found dead this morning, in a

garden farther down the road. She could have walked along Gypsy Lane some time after midnight. I've been sent to ask if you, or any of your household, saw or heard any movement about then?'

'I certainly didn't. I was in bed and asleep well before midnight. I can't answer for my wife. I say, this is a terrible thing. What was it, heart attack or something of the sort?'

'Could have been, sir. Perhaps I could check up with Mrs. Crane about last night? I won't keep her a minute.'

Crane smiled. 'She'll be hard at work by now — in Deniston. She runs a place in Nelson Street. Beauty parlour business. As the shop's fascia board has it, 'Anne.' Just that. But we could give her a ring. Yes, we'll do that. Will you come this way?'

Garrett followed him into a small, square, front hall, where a white telephone stood on a table. Over his shoulder Crane said, 'Better let me make the connection. I can get through to my wife, past her receptionist, quicker than you could. Agreeable?'

'Yes, sir, thanks. In fact, it might be easier if you put the question to her — about last night, you know. If you wouldn't mind?'

'Delighted.' Crane dialled, then began to speak crisply. 'That you, Hazel? Charles Crane here. Ask my wife to come to the telephone, please. It's urgent . . . Thanks . . . ' Then, 'Oh, Anne, darling. Now, don't be alarmed, it's quite all right — quite all right. But I have a policeman here, inquiring into the — er — sudden death of a local lady. It seems she was found in a garden and that she could have come down Gypsy Lane during the night. The police want to know if you saw or heard anything out of the ordinary then. That's all. Just that, nothing else.'

Garrett heard the faint crackle of a voice from the receiver, and Crane broke into it. 'No, I didn't imagine you would, any more than I did. That's it, then. 'Bye, darling.'

He replaced the receiver and turned to Garrett.

'Not a thing, officer. Sorry. It's a

shocking business, and a great pity we can't help you. But . . . ' he shrugged.

'That's the way it goes, sir.' Garrett swung his helmet by its strap. 'As I came through the yard just now I spoke to a man who was feeding the horses. He told me where to find you.'

'That would be — er — Frank.' Crane stuck his hands in his breeches pockets and looked at Garrett with his head cocked sideways. 'He wouldn't have much to say for himself, I expect?'

'He told me he was working here. He didn't sound like a local, though.'

'No. No, he isn't.' Crane shrugged again. 'He cast up here the other day and asked if there was a job going. As it happened, I was short-handed and was glad to take him on.'

'Does he live-in with you, sir?'

'Yes. We have a spare room and he seemed a decent sort of fellow. Too good for a shake-down in the barn, I mean.'

'Then I'd better have another word with him, sir, to check on last night.'

Crane nodded and stepped past him. 'I'll call him into the house.'

'It's all right, sir, I'll see him on my way out.' But Crane had gone quickly through the kitchen and was already in the yard. Garrett frowned, and followed him swiftly.

He found Crane in the barn, talking, quietly but rapidly, to his hired man. He looked up as Garrett paused in the doorway.

'He never heard a thing, officer, did you, Fred?' The black-haired young man shook his head and turned aside to pick up a wooden bucket. 'He slept like a log all night — like my wife and myself.'

Garrett walked slowly forward, feeling the tenseness of his leg muscles. 'All the same, we'd like a personal statement, sir.' He took a final, deciding look at Crane's helper. 'In fact, I think you'd better come along with me, hadn't you, Fred Mitchell?'

The young man shrank back against the bins, and his lips drew taut over clenched teeth. Garrett saw his eyes dart desperately from left to right and took a step nearer, reaching for his handcuffs.

'Don't try anything, Mitchell. The

district is just swarming with policemen. You wouldn't have a cat in hell's chance.'

Mitchell swallowed painfully. 'Look, copper, I never had anything to do with this dead woman. Never saw her, never heard of her.'

'You can tell — ' Garrett was beginning when Crane, who had been goggling at the pair of them, cut in hoarsely.

'What is all this? I don't understand.'

'I'm taking this chap in, sir. I've every reason to believe he is Fred Mitchell, who escaped from Leeds Prison three days ago.' He swung the handcuffs suggestively. 'What about these, Mitchell?'

'You can put 'em away. I shan't give trouble. And listen. Mr. Crane here knew nothing about it — who I am, I mean.'

'You can make a statement later. Let's go, Mitchell, lad. The governor at Leeds can't wait, I'll bet, to welcome you back to the old home.'

He walked at his capture's shoulder down Gypsy Lane. This was his lucky day, and he knew it.

4

Mr. and Mrs. Rennison, previously warned, had made preparations for their visitors. Hallam and Spratt were ushered into the lounge where a portable electric fire was burning. Mrs. Rennison, she of the dicky heart, was seated by the hearth, her husband had already set chairs for the policemen.

'Now, you won't want to be wasting time,' the old man said, 'So if there's anything we can tell you, though I'm afraid there isn't . . . '

Hallam absently noted the swift efficiency which produced Spratt's notebook and pencil in one unobtrusive movement.

'Did either of you hear anything unusual during the night?'

'I didn't,' Rennison said. 'I sleep like the dead.'

'Mrs. Rennison?'

'I didn't get off very soon last night. And I woke several times, couldn't exactly say when, though.'

'And all was quiet when you did wake, Mrs. Rennison? Think very carefully about that, please. Try and recollect every sound you heard from outside.'

Mrs. Rennison clasped her hands firmly in her lap and gazed at the ceiling for a full quarter-minute.

'Mr. Hall, at Number Twenty-three opposite, his car came in about eleven. He's a traveller and he often gets back late. Then I heard Mr. Levitt, from Twenty-seven, drive in soon after midnight. He and his wife play cards once a week with some friends in Hadley. And that was all.'

'You keep your front gates closed at night?' Hallam looked at the old man.

'We keep 'em closed all the time, sir.'

'And you think, Mrs. Rennison, if anybody had come through them while you were awake, you'd have heard them?'

She nodded vigorously. 'Certain of it.'

'Did you know the lady who was found in your garden?'

The couple exchanged glances.

'Well, not to say know,' Mrs. Rennison

answered. 'We knew who she was and where she lived. But I've never spoken to her and I don't think Tom has.' Rennison shook his head. His wife hesitated a moment. 'As a matter of fact, we didn't like her very much — I mean, we thought she was a bit nosy. She used to walk down Granville Road and when she passed our house she always seemed to be trying to peer through the windows. But I suppose I shouldn't be saying things like that about the poor soul now.'

Hallam didn't reply. He looked across at Spratt and the sergeant shook his head. Hallam got to his feet.

'I'm sorry this happened on your property,' he said. 'I expect you won't be very fond of that part of your garden for a while?'

Rennison shrugged. 'Won't bother us, sir. I saw worse, lots of times, in the First War. And the wife was a hospital nurse before I married her. I suppose you'll still be looking for clues up yonder?'

'Yes. I'll let you know when we've finished.' Hallam paused at the door. 'How long have you been living here?'

‘Ever since ’46. These houses were put up just before the last war, you see. We’d had our eye on this district to retire to, and this place was up for sale just right.’

‘Now, the Kayes next door. Have they been here long?’

‘About four years.’ Hallam caught the tautening of his voice, noted his change from loquacity to terseness.

‘He’s very nice,’ Mrs. Rennison said, ‘and we like the two little boys.’ She, too, brought her lips firmly together.

Rennison ushered them through the front door. Spratt said, ‘Hullo, what’s happening here?’ and they walked quickly forward. Garrett, backed by two of Hallam’s plainclothes men and a uniformed constable, was standing with a firm hand on the shoulder of a sullen-faced, black-haired young man.

‘What’s all this?’ Hallam demanded and, releasing his hold, Garrett saluted smartly.

‘Escaped prisoner, sir, from Leeds Prison. Frederick Mitchell. Found him at Crane’s riding-school.’

‘Did you indeed? You’ve done pretty

well for yourself, then.' Hallam thought quickly. 'Foster, you take him along to Division in one of the cars. This chap' — he nodded at the uniformed man — 'had better go with you. Tell Division to keep him there till I've talked to him, ask them, too, to let Leeds know. Get moving.'

He watched the police car drive away.

'Now, Garrett,' he said, 'let's have it — short and sweet.'

While Garrett described his visit to the Tanners, Spratt, his notebook supported on the gatepost, scrawled rapid shorthand. The young constable told of his meeting with Charles Crane and of his recognition of Mitchell.

'How did you get on to him so certainly?'

'It wasn't difficult, sir. The first time he saw me, he dodged back into the barn. I followed him in and I thought it a bit odd that he'd poured the sieveful of mixed feed he'd been carrying back into a bin of oats. That made me look at him again and I thought his features were familiar somehow — of course, I'd heard his description on my radio but that gave him as blonde. Crane first called him Frank, and then Fred. He — Crane, sir — had seemed anxious to talk to the chap before I could get a second go at him. But I followed him up, and then, because I was looking for it, I saw Mitchell's hair had been dyed black.'

'You think Crane knew who he was?'

'Mitchell made a point of swearing he didn't, sir. But there was that slip in the names, and Mrs. Crane runs a beauty-shop.'

Hallam shrugged. 'Not our pigeon to hook the Cranes for harbouring. Right, Garrett. You've done well, and I've no doubt it'll be credited. You'd better get back on patrol now.'

Garrett saluted again, straddled his motorcycle, spoke into his microphone and roared smartly away. Spratt closed his notebook.

'If I remember, Mitchell got five for robbery with violence, sir. D'you think that could help with this case?'

'I wouldn't bet on it. Suspect, yes, but no more at the moment, Jack. Let's go up the road and see where she lived.'

Number Eight was semi-detached with a neatly-formal front garden. The dead woman's key let them into a parquet-floored hall which smelt of recent polish.

They went quickly from room to room on the ground floor. Modern kitchen, small pantry, dining-room, lounge. Everything normal, nothing out of place.

'Upstairs, then,' Hallam said.

There were three bedrooms. Two were furnished, the third was full of boxes and household junk. Spratt put his head round the door of the front bedroom.

'She slept here, sir.'

'Yes.' Hallam joined him. 'Bed hasn't been slept in, of course. A neat and tidy person, wouldn't you say? Take the wardrobe, Jack. I'll see to this chest of drawers.'

They worked swiftly, and their fingers were surprisingly delicate as they probed among the femininities. They found nothing of interest, nothing out of the way. Hallam turned from the chest of drawers and squatted before a dual-shelved bookcase whose top made a bedside table. 'She claimed to be an ornithologist, you know, Jack, though young Garrett doubted it. If she had been, I'd have expected some bird books about the house.'

He straightened up and stepped to the window, peering out at the long, narrow back garden.

'Something odd here, sir,' Spratt said.

Hallam turned. The sergeant was pointing to a collection of objects set out along the mantelpiece over a fireplace filled with red tissue paper. 'What do you make of these, sir?'

'Matchbox, empty.' Hallam replaced it after an exploratory shake. 'Cigar stub, paper clip, a — er — tiddly-wink, isn't it? Button from a man's shirt, small twist of darning wool, lump of sugar. What do *you* make of them, Jack?'

'It's not them so much as the way they're set out, sir, all spread in order, like. Gives you the idea of a sort of collection almost. Maybe she was just one of these human squirrels?'

'Maybe.' Hallam frowned at the objects. 'Why a cigar stub? Shouldn't think she smoked them.' His hand went out as if to gather the motley pieces together, then he drew it back. 'No,' he said, 'not now. We'll go over this place again later. Let's get back down the road and see what's doing there.'

5

'Right.' Hallam dropped into his office chair, put a match to his after-lunch pipe and looked across at Spratt. 'Let's see what we've got so far.'

'We've got nothing from the garden, nor the lane, nor the wood,' Spratt began. 'I reckon the lads gave that wood, and the Common near it, a thorough going-over. If there'd been anything there, they'd have spotted it.

'Then there was the quick house-to-house we did in Granville Road. Again negative. Nobody saw Madge Adkin last night, nobody heard anything unusual. The late getters-in, Hall, the traveller, and the Levitts, couldn't help. Only Mrs. Mason, Tanner's sister, heard what she thought was a woman walking down Gypsy Lane. As for background, Madge Adkin lived alone, elder sister died eighteen months ago but Madge kept the house on. The two were daughters of a C.

of E. parson. Neighbours say Madge was a quiet, reserved person, friendly enough but not socially inclined. No money troubles apparently. All more negative stuff.

'On the other hand' — he tapped the book which lay on his desk — 'we've got this Scribbling Diary I found in the bureau downstairs when I had that second look through Madge Adkin's house. Haven't had a chance to study it properly but I'm hoping it'll be more helpful than the rest of the stuff in the bureau. And there's that collection of objects from the bedroom mantelpiece which I brought away. Also, we have got Fred Mitchell, late of Leeds Prisons. And there's that story of the row between Madge and Tanner.'

Hallam clicked his fingers. 'Meant to have another word with young Garrett before he went off duty.'

Spratt reached for the desk telephone. 'Might catch him in the canteen, sir.' He spoke into the instrument, put it down and returned to the job in hand.

'This looks to me like one of those

cases you'd run a mile to keep clear of, sir. I can feel it in my bones. Oh, yes, we've got Mitchell, and I know he was in for robbery with, but somehow I can't see Madge Adkin meeting him in the dark, recognizing him, and threatening to turn him in, so he did her. Can you?'

'Doesn't seem likely, Jack . . . You just mentioned Madge meeting somebody in the dark . . . I've been wondering — did she? Regularly?'

Spratt nibbled a thumb. 'You mean an affair, sir, with, say, one of the local married men? Could be. I'd say she was still attractive, in a way, and at that reckless age, too. Hell, sir, that's going to mean a fair bit of local digging, isn't it? And I hate those jobs. Like I said just now — '

He broke off as Garrett knocked and came in.

'Sorry to cut in on your off-duty time, lad,' Hallam said, 'but there are just one or two points. That jobbing-gardener, Tanner. Admitted he'd had a row with Miss Adkin, didn't he? Was he worried about it?'

'Not about the cat incident, sir. I mean, that obviously meant nothing to him. He treated it as a joke. But though he claimed it hadn't done him any harm, he hadn't liked Miss Adkin going around trying to damage his reputation as a gardener.'

'And Mitchell. You said you saw him as soon as you arrived at the riding-school. Did you tell him why you were there?'

'No, sir. I just asked where I could find Mr. Crane.'

'So you didn't mention Miss Adkin's death to him? You'd no chance of noting his reactions to that?'

'Crane told him, sir. Before I could get to Mitchell first, as I told you. And Mitchell denied he knew anything about it. When I brought him down the lane, all he seemed bothered about was what he'd get for making a break, sir.'

'I see. Now, you were first on the spot and you saw the Kayes. Any observations there?'

'Mr. Kaye was helpful, sir. Seemed a sensible, level-headed sort of chap. And I saw Mrs. Kaye, and the man who is staying there.' His voice slowed, hesitatingly, and Hallam's eyes held a sudden gleam of interest. But before he could urge the constable on, a knock at the door heralded a uniformed messenger who put a large envelope on Hallam's desk.

'Preliminary report from Forensic, sir. The Adkin case.'

'Thanks.' Hallam flicked the envelope across to Spratt and looked up at Garrett again. 'You were saying?'

'The Kayes' guest, sir. Pettifer. He didn't seem to fit in. Not the usual suburban type.'

'Well, you get all sorts, you know,' Hallam said absently. 'Right, Garrett, that's all for now.'

He picked up his telephone, asked the desk to have James Tanner brought in for questioning, and turned to Spratt. 'Well?'

'She wasn't killed where Kaye found her, sir. I sent in a specimen of soil from Rennison's garden, but there was none of it on her shoes. Fingernails clear, no signs of a struggle. She was strangled before she got that bump on the head, they think, but no evidence of sexual assault.

In fact, nothing helpful.'

Hallam grunted disgustedly. 'Dammit, there must be a line somewhere. Fetch Mitchell here, Jack. It's time we had a word with him.'

Mitchell was willing to talk, very anxious to put himself in the clear.

'Look, Inspector, I didn't see the woman, never mind touch her,' he said as soon as he was inside Hallam's office.

'Have you been accused of that, Mitchell?'

'No, but it stands to sense that's what you're thinking, with my record, doesn't it? And it stands to sense, too, I wouldn't do such a damn silly thing. I mean, where's the point?'

He looked from Hallam's impassive face to Spratt's.

'See, I'll tell you what happened. I saw the chance of a break and I took it. I was lucky — just then. Hell of a thunderstorm raging and the sky chucking it down. Nobody on the streets and if I was seen running, well, who wouldn't, to get out of that rain? Anyway, I've got a pal, see? Living not far from the can. He fixed me up and I hooked a lorry ride to this side of Deniston. That was last Friday. I called at a farm — I could take you to the place if you want me to prove it — asked if they'd got a job going. I mentioned I was used to horses and they told me to try Mr. Crane. Just my bleedin' luck your copper saw me.'

'And when did you dye your hair and eyebrows, Mitchell?'

'Oh, that? Oh, well, this pal in Leeds I told you about, he fixed me up.'

'You wouldn't care to give us his name and address?'

Mitchell snorted. 'That's a damn silly question, Inspector, and you know it. You can't make me, either.'

'Maybe not.' Hallam's lips twisted in a brief grin. 'Any more than I can prove — at the moment — that your story of a long dreamless sleep last night is the truth. But we'll soldier on. I'm sending you back to Leeds, Mitchell. I'll know where to find you if I want you again.'

He called the station desk and a constable came to escort Mitchell away.

Hallam said, 'Well, Jack?' Spratt shook his head.

'I don't see how she could have come across him, sir. Obviously, he'd be lying very low.'

'Yes. We'll have to talk to Crane . . . The man whose wife runs a beauty shop. Hair dyes and all that. I could do with knowing something about Mitchell's background. And where and how he did the jobs which hooked him.'

'I've looked that up, sir. He did a couple of smallish breaks on shopkeepers, which got him six months and then two years. Last time he flew a bit higher, slugged the proprietor of a Leeds garage as the man left his place to drop the day's takings into a night safe in the city. Mitchell dashed off with the loot and ran smack into the arms of a bobby just coming round the corner.'

'I see. Now, this chap Pettifer. Garrett remarked, as I did, that he doesn't fit in Granville Road. There's something odd about the set-up at that house . . . Well, we've got to start somewhere. Let's hope Tanner hands us a lead.'

James Tanner, dragged away from his jobbing gardening, and still in his working clothes, was inclined to complain of wasted time when he sat in the chair and faced Hallam across the desk.

'We're sorry to be a nuisance, Mr. Tanner,' Hallam said, 'but you must see this is a matter of importance. Now, you told the constable this morning — '

'All about the flare-up me and Miss Adkin had,' Tanner broke in. 'Oh, she was no pal of mine. But it wasn't me as did her in. I'd niver do such a thing as that.'

'The constable told you how she was killed, Mr. Tanner?'

'Come to think of it, he didn't. Just said she'd been killed, that's all.'

Hallam looked at the man's powerful hands and fingers.

'She was strangled,' he said briefly.

'Strangled? Nay, that's no way to die.' He shuddered.

Hallam glanced at the notes in front of him.

'Your sister, Mrs. Mason, heard footsteps — a woman's footsteps — in Gypsy Lane last night?'

'Aye. At a quarter after one.'

Hallam nodded. 'Now, we've some reason to believe Miss Adkin was in the habit of wandering around late at night. Did you know that?'

Tanner shook his head without reply.

'But, going about the estate, like you do in your work, you'll hear bits of gossip, comments and so on, I suppose? People will talk about their neighbours.'

'Not to me. I niver gossip. When I go to one of my customers, it's to work, not to talk.' He dug a watch from his waistcoat pocket and looked at its face. 'By gum!' he said significantly.

Hallam smiled. 'I've nearly finished, Mr. Tanner. And a police car will run you home. There's just one other thing. Miss Adkin was found in Rennison's garden, as you know. We're not convinced the killing took place there. We're wondering why that particular garden was chosen. I know there is a small gate leading into the lane. Is that common with those houses? I haven't had time to check on it yet.'

Tanner was suddenly alert, interested.

'See now. When the houses were put up

the builder gave 'em all split-chestnut fencing, six foot high, at the backs. There's one or two still has it — beastly ugly stuff, I reckon. Mostly, though, folks have done away with it. Some has beech hedges there, some privet. Two of the three detached houses, that's Furnisses and Kayes, have stone walls. I'd say roughly half of the gardens have gates at the back. They're handy for a short cut to the lane or if you want to dump garden rubbish there.

'Now, here's the point. Rennison's garden has a beech hedge and a little gate in one corner of it. Right?'

'Yes, we'd observed that.'

'Well, now. Next door, that's Mr. Benton's place, there's a privet hedge. Great overgrown gappy job, that is, and in the middle there's a space you could drive a hoss and cart through, just about. Benton's girl and her pals made that, playing there and in Ash Wood when they were nippers. Now' — he pointed a finger at Hallam — 'say Miss Adkin was down Gypsy Lane last night and say somebody did for her near the bottom of the lane and wanted to dump the poor soul in a garden, why bother with Rennison's gate when that monstrous big gap was close handy?'

'Could have been the killer didn't notice it in the dark,' Spratt suggested.

Tanner shook his head. 'It's a sight easier to spot nor Rennison's bit of a gate, even in the dark.'

Hallam pushed back his chair and rose. He was smiling.

'You see how useful a bit of local knowledge can be, Mr. Tanner.' He held out his hand. 'Thanks for coming along and talking to us.'

Tanner gripped his fingers in a quick squeeze which made Hallam wince.

'I hope you get the bloke responsible, sir,' he said.

'So?' Hallam said when the visitor had gone.

'Can't see it was him at the moment, sir,' Spratt replied. 'I don't reckon the motive was there. What was behind asking him about hearing gossip, sir?'

'I was thinking of the possibility of Madge Adkin meeting a lover at nights.

Tanner gets about the district, and though he doesn't reckon to listen to idle chit-chat, he'll hear plenty, I wouldn't wonder. But the fish didn't bite.'

He glanced at his office clock.

'See the Press Officer has the main facts about Mitchell, will you? That he has been retaken — Garrett's name can be mentioned. But keep the Cranes out of it for now. Say 'in the Ashwood district' only. And they can have what Adkin details there are. When you've done that, we'll have a run across to Dean Street.'

6

Deniston's civic pride lay in the modern design of its city centre with its shops and towering office blocks and in the continuing demolition of its former slums. The latter, now replaced by corporation estates and blocks of flats, formed the circumference of a circle separated from its centre by a band of tall Victorian terrace houses, ancient offices and abandoned churches and chapels which had now run shabbily to seed without yet reaching demolition point. Dean Street was part of this area.

'Cheap apartment houses, a couple of pubs, a few mouldering shops and a warren of one-man firms,' Spratt had described it to his Chief Inspector as he guided the police car expertly through the city-centre traffic.

The address they sought was a house in the middle of a long terrace, facing an area of waste ground which had once been gardens but was now a free car park. Spratt found a narrow space and squeezed into it; the two policemen advanced upon Number Sixty-three. There were area railings and broken steps leading to a basement. Beside them, a short flight of unswept stone steps gave access to an open hallway, its outer door set open and held back by a brick.

Alongside the door hung a slatted board which carried floor numbers and names. Hallam's glance travelled upwards by way of Benn Brothers, Brokers, F. Sowden, General Agent, The Quick-Service Mending Co., Carey and Walsh, Quality Printers, Gerald Herriot, and S. Pettifer, Healer.

'Third Floor,' he commented. 'What's 'Healer' mean, Jack?'

'Misprint, I reckon, sir,' Spratt said woodenly. 'Probably he nails on these shoe heels women are always losing.'

Hallam grunted and began to mount the stairs. At the top of the second flight some attempt had been made towards decency and order; a threadbare carpet replaced worn linoleum and the walls had been recently distempered. On the landing above were two doors, facing each other. They read, 'Gerald Herriot, Studio,' on one of them and 'Sidney Pettifer, Consulting Room,' on the other.

A drawing-pin, beneath 'Consulting Room' held a piece of roughly-torn paper against the wood. The policemen read, 'If closed inquire opposite or ring 183554' in shakily-printed capitals. Spratt knocked briskly on the door.

'Looks as if we'll have to inquire opposite,' he said after his second knock.

'Or ring 183554,' Hallam murmured. He had seen that number on the Kayes' telephone. They moved across the landing to the other door.

Their summons brought a man in his late twenties, as tall as they were and considerably heavier than either of them. He had fair hair and a pleasant, laughing face. He was dressed in a brown high-necked sweater, green cord slacks and tennis shoes. He looked them over and stepped aside.

'Come right in and tell me what I can do for you.'

The room had apparently several uses. There was a divan bed, a chest of drawers, an easy chair and a small desk at one end, a drawing board on a stand, an easel and a clutter of paints and brushes on a table at the other.

'Mr. Herriot?' Hallam asked formally and Spratt broke in when the young man nodded.

''Course it's Mr. Herriot, sir! Plays for the Hornets regularly, don't you? I see all your home games I can. That was a smasher last week, against Wareham. Never seen a better try scored than the one you put over, sir.'

Herriott shrugged modestly. 'Young Nobby handed it me on a beautiful plate. I couldn't have helped scoring even if I'd been running the other way.' He studied them again. 'Are you chaps police, by any chance? You have that air, you know.'

Hallam nodded. 'Detective Chief Inspector Hallam, sir. This is Detective Sergeant Spratt. We were hoping to have a word with Mr. Pettifer.' He jerked his head backwards.

'You were? And what's our Sid been doing?'

'Nothing, sir, as far as we are aware, but it's possible he might be able to help us with some inquiries we're making.'

Herriot said, 'We all fill this place so, standing up. The easy chair, Chief Inspector. And, Sergeant, if you don't mind the divan.' He propped himself against the desk when they were seated. 'Sorry I can't offer you anything. I'm teetotal and I don't smoke. Now, about Pettifer. He hasn't been around here for some time, as far as I know. In fact, I've wondered once or twice if he'd eloped with that fancy bit who's been hanging around his neck of late. I say eloped, because she's married. Anyway, there's a phone number on his door. Probably hers. You could get in touch that way.'

'You know Pettifer well, sir?'

'I know him, because we happen to live opposite each other. I try to be neighbourly — I mean, I agreed to deal with any inquiries for him. But we're not exactly bosom friends.'

'He lives here? It's not just his place of business?'

'No, this is his permanent address. He has a bed-sitter across the way, a twin to mine. You probably noticed the door opposite the head of the stairs — that's the kitchen-cum-bathroom we both share. Though I hardly ever meet him there, either cooking or washing.'

'What's this healer business of his, Mr. Herriot?'

'Well . . . Pettifer heals people — or claims to.'

'Has he any medical qualifications?'

'He took a course in massage by correspondence once, and has a highly-decorated certificate hanging on the wall to prove he passed.'

'But a masseur usually describes himself as such or possibly, in these days, as a physiotherapist. It's this 'Healer' idea which puzzles me,' Hallam complained.

'As far as I can gather, Chief Inspector, Sidney-boy does a bit of massage, a bit of faith-healing, a bit of naturopathy, and mixes them together. He reckons he has a vocation for making people better, a kind of gift for it, almost a magic touch. You should hear him talk! He doesn't need a publicity agent.'

'Does he make a living from his clients, would you say?'

Herriot shrugged. 'Oh, he gets a few people here and no doubt he does them some good. But he — well, he's a bit of a rough diamond. Not likely to attract a good-class clientele. And, apart from a rubbing couch — not a very clean one, either — and an anatomical wall chart, he hasn't the usual physiotherapist's apparatus. In short, he runs on a shoe-string and a knotted-up one at that. He's tried to touch me more than once, but trying was as far as he got. He handed me that line about his vocation and his wonderful gift, but the truth, I fancy, is that he doesn't like work. Look, I've been shooting my mouth off fairly, haven't I? But as you're police . . . Citizen's duty, and all that . . . I hope I won't be quoted officially on all this?'

'Oh, no, sir,' Hallam assured him. 'We're not taking notes. You read the evening paper?'

'Sure.'

'There'll be a report in it tonight of the death of a woman in the Ashwood district. Pettifer is staying there at the moment and though we've no reason to believe he is implicated in any way, we have to make the routine check of everybody in the vicinity of the incident, you understand.'

'You don't say?' Herriot's eyebrows shot up. 'Ashwood, eh? I thought Sidney-boy was batting on a good wicket nowadays. Would he be living, by any chance, with a well-proportioned blonde, a trifle passee but still hot stuff?'

'He's a guest in the house of a lady who might merit that description, Mr. Herriot. Do you know her?'

'I've met her. She turned up here several weeks ago, in a blue Zephyr, looking for him. Pettifer was out having lunch. I ran into her on the stairs and she said she wanted to consult him professionally. I knew he'd soon be back, and he'd locked his place up, of course, so I invited her to step in here. Blow me backwards, Chief Inspector! Within five minutes she was hinting strongly that if ever I needed a model, she'd be only too pleased. I told her sorry, but I didn't use 'em, to which she replied it was never too late to start. By that time she was calling me Gerry — she'd seen the name on the door, of course — and urging me to call her Stella. I tell you, I was damn glad when Pettifer turned up and took her off my hands. That high-pressure stuff from women always bores me rigid.'

'She was satisfied with Mr. Pettifer's methods of treatment, it seems.'

'Certainly was. She started coming twice, and then three times a week. I ribbed him about it, of course, and he looked smug and said he reckoned his ship had come in at last.'

Hallam rose. 'Thank you, Mr. Herriot. We'll leave you to it.' He strolled across to the drawing board. 'Ah, commercial artist, I see.'

'Yes. I prefer that way of life to the family business.'

'They tell me you're one of the heavy-engineering Herriots, sir,' Spratt put in.

‘That’s right. My two elder brothers run the business since Father retired. I live in this crummy dump because it’s cheap, and I’ve got to prove I can make a living this way, you see.’

When they returned to Headquarters, Hallam spent a couple of hours at his desk, clearing his In tray. Then, at half-past five, he rang for Spratt.

‘Nothing new in about the Adkin job, Jack? Well, we’ll knock off, I think. We’ll have to go all out on it tomorrow. Perhaps, if we come fresh at it then . . . ’

7

On the following morning Hallam let loose a squad of half-a-dozen plainclothes men, headed by Spratt, upon Granville Road. Discreetly and without forcing the issue, they were to find out all that Granville Road people could tell them of Madge Adkin and her habits.

Hallam sat in his car for some minutes, watching his men going about their business before he let the car run quietly down the slope of Granville Road towards the Kayes' detached house. He left the car outside the gates and walked along the drive past the front door to the side door which gave into the kitchen.

His hand was raised to knock when he became aware of some sort of scuffle going on within. The kitchen window adjacent to the door was open and through it came Stella Kaye's voice.

'Stop it, Sid!' The admonition was accompanied by a giggle. 'Leave me alone! It's much too early in the day for that!'

Hallam knocked sharply, there was silence and then the woman's voice again.

'Oh, hell! Who can that be?'

But when she opened the door and saw Hallam there, her face was at once full of welcome. Her hands went up to her hair.

'Chief! How lovely to see you again! Come right in — we're just making coffee.'

She was wearing a thin housecoat, somewhat insecurely belted, and pom-pom slippers. Hallam judged there was very little clothing, if any, under the housecoat.

He nodded to Pettifer who was lounging on a kitchen chair. The big red-haired man, who had not shaved that morning and was still collarless, returned his acknowledgement with a surly 'How do,' which left the addition of 'copper' hanging markedly behind his lips.

Stella Kaye put a scarlet-nailed hand on Hallam's arm, drawing him forward. 'Let's go into the lounge, and you can tell me all the latest. Sidney'll make the coffee and bring it in to us.'

Hallam thanked her, followed her into the lounge. The settee had been pushed back from the fire and a line of four cushions was spread out on the hearthrug. There was something else, too, a two-foot length of malacca cane which Stella Kaye picked up quickly and pushed down at the back of the settee.

'Please excuse the muddle,' she said, 'but Sidney has been giving me a treatment. We just broke off for our elevenses.' She patted an easy chair, saw Hallam seated and, gathering up the cushions, arranged them on the settee before she sank gracefully upon it.

'Treatment?' Hallam repeated. 'You're not well, Mrs. Kaye?'

She made a tiny grimace. 'Why not 'Stella?' I hate the formalities. About the treatment. You see, I wasn't at all well some time ago. So I went to see Dr. Iverson, and he examined me everywhere' — she cast her eyes down demurely — 'and said I had a touch of muscular rheumatism. Well, I mean to say, rheumatism, at my age! Of course I took the pills he gave me but they did no good and I became pretty desperate.' She laced her fingers behind her head and crossed her legs. Hallam suppressed a grin. He'd seen that calculated move before, many a time. The upflung arms stretched the house-coat, pulling its skirts apart, so that the crossed legs showed the knees and a goodly area of nakedness above them. He was conscious of Stella Kaye's under-lashed glance at him but his stony stare at her face gave no indication that he was aware of the manœuvre.

'Anyway, to cut a long story short, Chief, I was getting worse and worse and then I heard of Sidney Pettifer from a friend and consulted him. He's done wonders for me — sheer wonders. He's an amazing man, you know. He has a marvellous gift of healing. I only wish he were better known.'

'He has cured your trouble?'

'Almost. But I have to have a session with him at least once a day and sometimes twice, so the only thing to do was — '

She broke off at a rattle of china

outside. Jumping up and tightening the belt at her waist, she opened the door to let Pettifer in. A cigarette, dangling from his lips, spilled ash into one of the coffee cups on the tray he carried. Stella Kaye brought a low table forward, Pettifer put his tray upon it, fished out the floating ash with a nicotine-stained, black-nailed forefinger and, picking up one of the other cups, moved to the chair opposite Hallam's.

'Sid!' Stella Kaye spoke reprovingly.

'Oh, sorry!' He put the cup back and carried the tray across to her. With a glance at Hallam which flaunted, he thought, a measure of defiance, Mrs. Kaye took the cup which had received the ash and stirred brown sugar into it. Hallam nodded his thanks as he took the third cup.

'I met a friend of yours yesterday, Mr. Pettifer,' he said casually. 'Mr. Gerald Herriot.'

'Oh, you did, didya? You mean you was nosing round my place, I s'pose? Take yer skeleton keys with yer?'

Hallam continued to stir his coffee.

'Now, now, Mr. Pettifer,' he replied mildly. 'You know we don't do things like that. It's easier, and much more comfortable, to get a search warrant.'

'What was you doing there, then?'

'Just making routine inquiries.' Hallam smiled pleasantly over his raised cup.

But Pettifer wasn't saying any more. He stubbed his cigarette hard into an ashtray, took a gulp of coffee and stared at the rug at his feet.

Stella Kaye broke the pause.

'Well, now,' she said briskly. 'What's to do, Chief? Have you come to tell me you've got your man?'

'I wish I had, Mrs. Kaye. However, we have some evidence which points to Miss Adkin being alive at a quarter past one. As far as we can gather, you and Mr. Pettifer here were the only people in Granville Road still not in bed at that time. Also, Miss Adkin's body was found in the next garden to yours. Now, I know you have both said you heard nothing unusual, but I would like you to consider that again. If you could dig really deep into your memories they might come up with something. It does happen.'

Stella Kaye, her feet discreetly together now, played noiselessly with her coffee spoon, her eyes misted with concentration. Pettifer continued to stare unmovingly. Then the woman sighed.

'I'm sorry. I can't recollect a single thing.'

'Nor me,' Pettifer grunted.

'Let's see if a little reconstruction will help,' Hallam suggested. 'Mr. Kaye had gone up to bed soon after eleven. Mrs. Kaye, you and Mr. Pettifer sat up talking. Until two o'clock. The lights were on and the curtains were drawn in this room — yes? Right. Were you making general conversation or discussing some particular subject?'

Stella Kaye flashed a glance at Pettifer and answered quickly.

'Sidney gave me a treatment first — I've told the Inspector I'm under your professional care, Sid — because we can concentrate on it better when there's no chance of interruptions. That took about an hour. Say until twelve. Then we had a break and a cigarette and then . . . Then we just talked of this and that.'

'Until you went to bed. Now, Mr. Pettifer, your bedroom faces over the back garden here. Were the curtains drawn?'

'They was.'

'Did you go to the window, to adjust it, say?'

Pettifer paused in the act of taking another cigarette from a crumpled packet.

'Come to think of it, I did. I ain't one o' these fresh-air fans, and it were blowing in a bit cool. An' now I remember I stood looking out a few seconds afore I shut it. I told you, didn't I, as I thought as I'd heard somebody moving about outside some nights previous? The thought crossed me mind again and I had me a bit of a listen, like. But nothing doing at all.'

Hallam levered himself upright. 'That could be helpful. It affects the time-element, anyway. Thanks for the coffee — most enjoyable.'

He found Spratt sitting in the car he had left outside.

'Well, we've just about covered it again,

sir. I've sent the gang back to H.Q.'

'Any luck?'

'Nothing on Madge Adkin. But one woman opened up considerably on the subject of Mrs. Kaye. Name of Pelling. Young Sutton interviewed her. I think you'll be interested to hear his report.'

8

Detective Constable Sutton stood before Hallam's desk and presented his report.

'In the course of my house-to-house inquiries in Granville Road, sir, I called upon a Mrs. and Miss Pelling. I did not introduce the subject of Mrs. Kaye myself, as I had no instructions to do this. Miss Pelling is, I judge, in her middle forties, she works as a secretary to Dalys, the brewers, and lives with her aged mother at Number Seventeen, Granville Road.'

'Yes?' Sutton had come to a stop and seemed to need nudging on.

'Miss Pelling, who was not at work today, sir, claimed to be a close friend of the deceased Miss Adkin, who saw her regularly. She — Miss Pelling — happened to mention to Miss Adkin a visit she had paid, in connection with her employment, to a public house, the 'Merry Piper' in Dean Street. She saw

Mrs. Kaye there, drinking with the red-haired man who is at present living at the Kayes'. The time was two o'clock in the afternoon when, according to Miss Pelling, no lady would be seen propping up a public bar and making eyes at the landlord, especially if unescorted by her husband.'

'So?'

'Miss Pelling told Miss Adkin this and Miss Adkin said the goings on at the Kayes' house were disgraceful, and should be stopped for the children's sake if nothing else. And Mrs. Pelling added that Miss Adkin was quite right. Mrs. Kaye was a blot on the district, the way she and that man were carrying on, and nobody around could understand what the husband was doing to allow it. And that's all, sir,' Sutton ended, more hurriedly now, 'only my instructions were to note and report anything at all out of the ordinary.'

'Which you have done,' Hallam agreed. 'And thanks.'

He swivelled his chair to face Spratt's smaller desk in the corner as the door closed behind Sutton. 'Can't make much out of all that, I think.'

Spratt shrugged. 'Pettifer's not a Granville Road type. We've agreed on that ourselves. Bound to be a bit of gossip over the back fences about him and the Kayes. Probably this Pelling spinster and her mother just happen to be the types who'd bring it up to one of our lads.'

'And Miss Pelling was Madge Adkin's friend. So . . . Just a minute, Jack. Supposing Madge did worry about the effect on the Kaye children of their mother having an affair with Pettifer — if she is having one — and felt compelled to tackle those two about it? Suppose she went to Kaye's place via Gypsy Lane early yesterday morning, walked to the house through the back garden and — Hell, that won't do . . . Kaye has a solid wall between his land and Gypsy Lane. Unless she was prepared to do some climbing and plunging about other people's gardens in the dark . . . No, hardly likely.'

'She could have walked down the street to the house, though.'

‘Possibly. Then who was the woman Mrs. Mason, Tanner’s sister, heard going down Gypsy Lane? Until we know to the contrary, we’ve got to assume that was Madge Adkin. What’s more, even if she had pitched into Pettifer and Mrs. Kaye, and Pettifer had lost his temper . . . I wonder . . . What’s biting you?’

Spratt had come quickly across the room to seize the case file which lay on Hallam’s desk.

‘Where’s that Forensic report? Ah — shoes . . . shoes. No, she didn’t put a foot on Kaye’s drive, after all. I noticed it had been newly tarmacadamed with a fairly loose top surface, not all worked in yet. There’d be some of that stuck to the crepe rubber soles she was wearing, if she went that way. It’s not mentioned — soles showed dust from the lane only.’

Hallam sprang up abruptly. ‘We’ll get nothing at all, sitting here. We haven’t seen the Cranes yet. We can’t rule out Fred Mitchell as a possibility, I suppose. And that Pettifer, confound him, keeps popping up in my mind. I wonder if he has a record, by any chance?’

Spratt shook his head. 'I've checked that. But if you'd like to find out a bit more about him, sir, we could try that pub in Dean Street he apparently uses. The 'Merry Piper,' where Miss Pelling saw him with Mrs. Kaye.'

'It isn't easy to get a landlord to talk about his customers.'

'We might be able to work it with this one, sir.' Spratt grinned mysteriously, picked up the telephone and asked for an outside line. He dialled a number already noted on his desk pad. Hallam heard the telephone's muted calling and a man's voice answering it. Spratt sat up alertly.

'Alf Lister? This is your old school pal, Jack Spratt.'

The telephone boomed in astonishment and pleasure.

'Yes,' Spratt answered. 'I'm doing all right. Detective Sergeant now, Alf. Aye, I was on a job with my chief inspector in Dean Street yesterday and spotted your name on the board. Hadn't time to call in then. How are things with you?'

Hallam gathered things weren't too bad at all.

'That's fine, Alf. Well, look. We're making some inquiries and you may be able to help us . . . No, nothing to do with your trade at all. If we could come along . . . Just a minute.' He pressed the mouthpiece to his shoulder and looked at Hallam. 'Straightaway, sir? They've just closed, so it would be a convenient time.' Hallam nodded. 'Yes, Alf, that'll be fine. We'll be along in a few minutes. My love to Kate . . . Oh, will she? That's great!'

He cradled the receiver. 'Alf Lister and I were at school together, sir. He married a girl who lived next door to me. We've drifted apart a bit over the years.'

But lapse of time and broken communication had done little to weaken Alf Lister's delight at meeting his old friend again. He let his visitors in by the side door of the inn, a big man in his shirt sleeves, round and red of face, with a hearty voice and a deep belly laugh to go with it.

'Come and meet the missus, Chief Inspector,' he invited. 'Jack here knows her already — matter of fact, if I hadn't nipped in before him . . . But that's going back a few years. You'll join us in a cup of tea. We always brew up as soon as we've closed for the afternoon.'

He showed them into a room at the back, a small, sunny place furnished with taste and some degree of elegance. Kate Lister, a handsome, well-fleshed blonde, held out both hands to Spratt over the low table which held the tea things.

'George! How lovely! And you haven't changed a bit!'

'You took those words from my own mouth, Kate. And it's worth the visit to hear my proper christian name again. Even my wife calls me Jack.'

Hallam sat back and sipped his tea, relaxing outside the flood of do-you-remembers and what-happened-to-old-So-and-so? Not waste of time entirely. Spratt was softening these two up, oiling the lock before he pushed in the key.

But Hallam knew he could trust Spratt not to make too big a meal of it, and as soon as he saw his chance, the sergeant broke into the reminiscences.

'We could go on all night, I'll bet. And some time, when I'm off duty, that's just what we will do.'

'Of course,' Lister assented readily. 'You're here on business, aren't you?'

Hallam smiled. 'We're not here for anything very serious. We're just checking up on a few people known to have been in the vicinity of a case we're on. One of them is a man named Pettifer. Sidney Pettifer.'

Kate Lister opened large blue eyes and her chin came up as she stared at her husband.

'Oh, him,' the publican said drily.

'We know he lives across the street. We know he's been seen in your bar. Regular customer?'

Lister's mouth twisted derisively. 'I could do without him. I'm not supposed to keep a slate — that's brewery rules, but as you know, there are times when we have to give credit. Pettifer's never been into my ribs for anything more than a pound or two, but he's one of these who'll never clean his account up. He hasn't been in lately, by the way.'

'Do you know anything about him, apart from his being a customer?'

'I know lots.' Lister snorted. 'So does everybody else who's ever been within ten yards of him in my bar. Proper bigheaded blabbermouth. Reckons to have a wonderful gift of healing, only a hard world won't recognize his talent. All that. You can have him for me, Mr. Hallam. But what's he been doing to have you two on his track?'

'Nothing, as far as we know, Mr. Lister. Of course, this visit to you is confidential, as I know you'll appreciate. But yesterday morning a woman was killed — '

Kate Lister's cup rattled into its saucer.

'Oh, my God!' she said breathlessly. 'Not Dora North?'

Her husband laughed shortly. 'Of course not, love. Dora's all right. Came into the bar, she did, just before closing. They'd run out of change again. You're on about that woman up at Ashwood, aren't you, Mr. Hallam? Kate never reads newspapers.'

'Yes. Pettifer is staying in the district, we're checking up on everyone there. But what's this about a Dora North?'

'You tell it.' Lister gestured to his wife.

'Dora works as a waitress in the Kumfi Kafe, just down the street from here. She's knocking on thirty, rather striking looking — black hair, very dark eyes. Gypsy type. She's single. Well, she got to know Sidney Pettifer, or he got to know her, have it which way you like. Started taking her out. Then this woman — a new patient — came along. A right posh piece in a big car. She was coming regularly for — oh, must have been a fortnight or three weeks. Then one night, as we were getting ready for bed — I was upstairs and Alf was cashing up — I heard the very devil of a row going on outside our back yard. Man and woman at it hammer and tongs. It was Dora and Pettifer. Naturally, being me, I opened the window quietly and had a good listen. It seems Dora had waited for him at closing time and had got him round there to tell him the facts of life. It was all about this posh blonde, and what Dora was going to do to her if he didn't cut free from her. She said she'd find out where this bitch lived and claw her eyes out. That sort of thing. I was just going to call Alf to go and break it up when Dora suddenly rushed away, crying. He went back across the way, home, I suppose.'

'I see. D'you think they made it up afterwards?'

'That I couldn't say. As Alf's told you, Dora comes in here now and then. She hasn't said anything to you, has she, Alf?'

'No. In fact, she seems to have gone all quiet, like, recently. I've seen this blonde myself, Mr. Hallam. He's brought her in, afternoon times, for a drink more than once.'

'Married woman, Mr. Lister?'

'That's right. He called her Stella. They seemed to be very friendly, too.'

Hallam put his hands on the arms of his chair. 'Well, Jack . . . '

'Just a minute.' The landlord leaned forward. 'I'm not trying to get anybody into trouble, mind, but — You say you're checking up on Pettifer in connection with that Ashwood case. Right. Well, I reckon you ought to talk to a pal of mine. Ted Walsh. He runs a little printing business on the floor beneath Pettifer's place across yonder. If you like, we'll go over and I'll introduce you to Ted.'

Edward Walsh was small, dried-up and elderly. He wore a stained apron and peered at his visitors with faded blue eyes behind rimless spectacles. There was hardly room for the four of them in the tiny office into which he invited them. A battered desk in one corner held a telephone and order books, there were two tall filing cabinets and a range of shelves carrying assorted piles of paper and card.

'Workshop's through there,' Walsh said, an inky thumb indicating a closed door. 'Work on me own here now. Cary, me partner, died last year.'

'Business good, Mr. Walsh?' Hallam asked sociably.

'Can't grumble. Might do better in better premises, but then there's rent and rates. Wicked in the city centre. Well, Alf?'

'The Chief Inspector would like to hear what you told me about Pettifer and that girl, Ted.' The publican jerked his chin ceilingwards. 'In confidence, Ted, they want to know all they can about your upstairs neighbour.'

'Right.' Walsh leaned back against the

desk. Hallam liked his sharp, decisive manner, his economy of words.

'Don't see much of Pettifer. Fairly quiet, too, mostly. But about a fortnight ago I was working late. Rush order. Hell of a row started upstairs — girl's voice screaming, Pettifer shouting back. I knew Mr. Herriot was out, and I didn't like that screaming. Went upstairs to the landing. Heard the girl crying out — 'No! Stop it, Sid! You're murdering me!' Voice sounded sort of strangled. Was this where I bust in? Stood dithering there and I heard him tell her to get out, and stop out. So I nipped smartly down here. Heard the door open. He said, 'I'll go where I like and with who I like, and I'm warning you, you hell-cat, stay away from me!' Opened me door a crack and peeped out. Girl came running down, sobbing, clutching her throat. Girl from the cafe across the street. Upset, I was. Finished me job and went over to Alf's for a drink. He asked me what was up. I told him.'

'Of course,' Lister said, 'when I told the

missus she said so what? Just a lovers' tiff. But I'd seen Ted here, and how shook-up he was.'

Walsh wagged his head.

'No ordinary quarrel, that. Girl was hurt bad. Sure of it.'

His mouth clamped into a thin line and Hallam knew he'd said his piece. He thanked the printer, and, on the pavement outside, Spratt and he took a warm leave of Alf Lister.

'Aren't we seeing this Dora North now we're here, sir?' Spratt asked as Hallam turned towards their parked car.

'Not at the moment, Jack. We've got an objective picture. Pettifer starts making a fuss of this girl, all goes well till Mrs. Kaye comes along. She takes Pettifer up in a big way and Dora naturally kicks up. Hence the rows we've heard about. Now, let's see how that objective picture fits into the Adkin job, if it does. Later on, we can get Dora's story, if that proves necessary. We'll have the subjective stuff from her.'

Spratt nodded. 'Of course. She'll either accuse him of every crime in the statute book or else, if she's still in love with him, she'll whitewash and alibi him from here to Christmas.'

'I shouldn't wonder.' Hallam settled himself into the car. 'The one and only thing certain about our job, Jack, is that you can never tell with women.'

9

Charles Crane signalled with an uplifted arm to the teenage girl who was riding in the paddock.

'Christine! Time to come in now, please!'

He saw his pupil's irritated shrug but she pulled her pony hard round and kicked it into a canter. Watching her come up to the gate, Crane's mouth curled in a grimace of disgust. This tall girl with the bad-tempered lips and the lank, fashionably-untidy hair, riding in jeans and a sloganed sweater — by God, what hideous messes they made of themselves nowadays!

She rode into the yard, flung herself off and turned to Crane.

'I can't stop to see to him tonight,' she said abruptly. 'I've got too much home-work to do. Besides' — there was calculated insolence in her tone now — 'daddy says he doesn't see why we should be expected to groom a horse after we've had to pay for riding it.'

Crane kept his temper. 'You don't only come here to ride, Christine. You tell me you're hoping to have a pony of your own someday. Looking after that pony is something you have to learn, too, isn't it?'

The girl shrugged again, disinterestedly.

'Grooming your own pony's different from having to muck about with somebody else's. Daddy says — '

'Right. You can tell your father from me you won't be coming here any more. Tell him also I shall be pleased to have a settlement of my account with him for your lessons. It's been outstanding long enough.'

He walked Craddles, the pony, quickly towards the stables. A tall, rangy man of early middle age was standing in the yard, looking about him. Crane raised his free hand.

'Be with you in a moment.' He led the pony to a loose box, frowning at the foam on its neck and withers. Slipping off saddle and bridle, he flung a rug over the sweating beast and left it with a well-filled hay net. In the yard, his visitor, a quizzical look in his eyes, watched Christine marching out through the drive gates.

'Young lady seems upset,' he remarked.

'She's just had the last lesson she'll ever get from me. I can't afford to turn pupils away, but I'll have no impertinent ham-handed young bitches telling me what to do. You were looking for me?'

'If you are Mr. Charles Crane, yes, sir. Detective Chief Inspector Hallam, Deniston C.I.D.'

Crane sighed. 'I've been expecting a visit from you people. About Fred Mitchell, I suppose? Right, we'll go into the house. My wife's due back from business any minute. You'll want to see her, too, no doubt.'

Hallam followed him into the house along a short passage to a room which smelt of leather and tobacco. There was a handsome desk in the middle of the fitted carpet, sporting prints and photographs of horses and hounds covered the walls. Crane gave Hallam a deep leather chair at one side of the fireplace. He switched on the electric fire before he sat down opposite.

'Do light up, if you wish, Chief Inspector. I'll join you.'

He lifted a worn briar from the mantelpiece and began to fill it slowly from an oak jar emblazoned with a college shield. He waited until Hallam had his own pipe going.

'Now,' he invited, 'tell me the worst. What do we get for harbouring a man on the run?'

'And attempting to assist him to escape re-arrest, sir?'

'There were mitigating circumstances. I suppose I'll have to tell you the facts, unless you know them already?'

'I'm not here for that purpose, sir. It's no concern of mine. If there are proceedings against you, that's solely in the hands of the Director of Public Prosecutions.'

'But you said — '

'You brought the subject up, sir. No, I'm investigating the death of Miss Madge Adkin only.'

Crane looked relieved. 'I'm afraid I

can't be of much help there. As I've already told your constable, neither my wife nor I heard or saw anything on the night she was killed.'

'You knew Miss Adkin?'

Crane shook his head.

'It seems she was accustomed to walk in Gypsy Lane late at night. Did you ever see anyone there at such a time?'

'Can't say I did.' Crane cocked his head sideways. 'Ah, that's my wife's car. Would you like to have her join us?'

'Yes, please.'

Hallam was on his feet when Anne Crane entered. She was tall, she was beautifully dressed and impeccably complexioned. Neither handsome nor pretty, Hallam decided, but attractively halfway between the two. And a good advertisement for her own profession as a beautician.

She bowed in response to her husband's introduction, and, stripping off her driving gloves, took his chair. Crane perched on the big desk. Mrs. Crane braced herself.

'Is it about Fred?'

'No, Mrs. Crane. As I've just told your husband, I'm here on entirely different business. But Fred Mitchell seems to be on both your minds.'

'He is my step-brother,' Anne Crane said hurriedly. 'But I expect you know that. You'll have gone into his background records.' Hallam hadn't, but he permitted himself a brief omniscient smile. 'I promised to look after him,' she went on, 'when mother died — his father was killed in a road accident not long after my mother's second marriage — but, obviously, I didn't make a very good job of it. Anyway, I've helped him out of trouble once or twice, and when he turned up here the other day, what could I do? He was hoping to get abroad, and Charles agreed he could stay here until things cooled off a bit and arrangements could be made. I dyed his hair and eyebrows. Look, Mr. Hallam, Fred isn't all bad and he certainly hadn't anything to do with that poor woman's death.'

'It's a fact he tried his best to shield you two — swore you didn't know he was a man on the run. I've talked to him, and

I really can't see any valid reason why he should have had anything to do with Madge Adkin. But I've no proof she didn't meet him, and recognize him, and until I have, I'm keeping him in mind. So we know where we are now, and if I may, I'll go back to the point we'd reached when you arrived, Mrs. Crane.'

But Anne Crane, also, could give him no information on Madge Adkin's night-wanderings.

Hallam picked up the pipe he had put down at Mrs. Crane's entrance and studied it.

'In confidence, I may tell you there's a possibility Miss Adkin was meeting a man in Gypsy Lane — '

'Ah!' Mrs. Crane's exclamation cut across his words like a sword. Hallam looked up at her sharply.

'Yes, Mrs. Crane?'

'About three weeks ago, latish at night, Charles went across to the stable to have a look at a mare which wasn't at all well. He had gone out of the side door and had left it open. I heard a couple in the lane having a terrific row. My curiosity got the better of my good manners, I'm afraid. I walked quietly round the house and stood in the shadow of the front porch. The man was telling the woman to clear out and leave him alone, he was angry, and then he suddenly changed his tone and put on a pleading note. He said something like, 'Don't queer my pitch, love. I'm on to a good thing here. And you're right off beam thinking what you do about it. Give us a chance till I see how it all turns out.' But the woman wasn't having that. She became abusive and referred to some third person as just a cheap tart. The man walked away from her then, down the lane. She stood for a few seconds before she turned in the opposite direction and made for the main road. I didn't discuss the incident with Charles when he came in. I was rather ashamed I'd been eavesdropping.'

'Could you identify these people, Mrs. Crane?'

'Oh, no. It was a very dark night. The woman spoke with rather an uneducated accent. So did the man.'

'The woman hardly sounds like Miss Adkin.'

'I wouldn't know about that. I've never spoken to her.'

Hallam rose to go. 'Thanks for telling me, anyway. I won't take up any more of your time. And don't worry too much about helping your step-brother, Mrs. Crane. I can't make any promises, of course, but there's a good chance the authorities may decide to be lenient.'

He refused the drink Crane offered him and walked slowly down Gypsy Lane. It was a quiet, mellow autumn evening with the dusk closing in quickly now. But Hallam was in no mood to appreciate nature's beauties nor its solaces. He was badly stuck on this case, and he knew it.

The quick, regular snapping of the jaws of a pair of shears broke into his gloomy musings. He came to a privet hedge bordering the lane. Behind it, a dumpy man with round spectacles was working busily.

'Good evening,' Hallam called out. 'You'll need a light soon.' He marked the gap in the middle of the hedge of which

Tanner, the jobbing gardener, had spoken. The owner — what was the name Tanner had used? Bowles? Bailey? No, Benton — was tackling the hedge at long last.

'Yes, yes.' Benton peered at him. 'I don't get much time for gardening.' He stepped closer and stared over the untidily-snagged branches. 'Aren't you a policeman? I saw you dodging about here yesterday, I believe.'

'I am from the Deniston C.I.D., sir.'

'Are you now?' His tone was cuttingly dry. 'Well, you might give a message from me, as a ratepayer, to the official in charge of the case, whoever he is.'

'That would be Chief Inspector Hallam, sir.'

'Then you can tell him from me — my name is Benton, by the way — to pull his finger out and use his brains. Obviously, there's a madman lurking in the district. It's the only explanation for that poor woman's death. And as the father of a teenage daughter —Yes, what is it, Christine?'

Hallam could just make out the lank, ungainly figure which had come up the garden.

'Mummy says how much longer are you going to be? Dinner will be spoiled if she leaves it much longer.'

'Right.' Benton swung back for a final thrust across the hedge. 'Madman — homicidal maniac — don't forget that, my man. And if something isn't done about it very soon, there'll be an exceedingly strong letter in the paper, over my signature!'

'Yes, sir,' Hallam replied meekly. 'I'll see the Chief Inspector gets the message, sir.'

He strolled on to the end of the lane, where it petered out on to Granville Common. He turned right at the corner of Reginald Kaye's property and headed up Granville Road. The street lights had sprung to life, most of the front windows of the houses were glowing, and the home-coming cars swung off the main road behind dual beams. As Hallam passed Kaye's gates, he saw a well-kept Zephyr standing on the drive. Beyond it, the dining-room was brightly lit though the curtains were not drawn. The table was set for an evening meal and Pettifer was already seated, his elbows on the table, his head bent over a newspaper. Hallam's pace slowed as Stella Kaye came into the room, carrying a plate of bread. She put it on the table near Pettifer, then ruffled his gingery-red hair as she turned away. Pettifer swung half round, caught her wrist with one hand and her fingers with the other. He bent the fingers back and Hallam saw the woman's mouth open in an expostulating 'Ow!' of pain. Very nice, very intimate, quite lover-like, Hallam thought, hurrying on now to the main road, where he had left his car.

He had parked near a telephone kiosk. He went in, dialled his C.I.D. Headquarters.

'Sergeant Manningham,' the instrument announced.

'Hi, Manny. Hallam here. Anything special for me?'

'There's a young woman wants to see you, sir. Name of Dora North. She said something about a man Pettifer.'

Hallam groaned inwardly. He'd planned to take a short cut home from Ashwood Road.

'Can you take a statement from her?'

'She won't give one. Says she must see you personally. First thing tomorrow, if not tonight.'

'Right. In that case, tell her nine o'clock in the morning.'

He put the receiver down, and, with a sigh of relief, returned to his car and set his face for home.

10

On the following morning, a Thursday, Hallam reached his office at eight-forty. The duty sergeant wished him good morning and told him Dora North had already arrived.

'Her appointment is for nine, Patterson. I'll ring for her when I've had a look at the mail.'

He ran through the contents of his In tray, which held nothing of moment except a request to confer with his Chief Superintendent and the Assistant Chief Constable at two o'clock that afternoon. Hallam frowned at the invitation, grunting a good morning to Spratt as his sergeant came breezily in.

'We're for the high jump with the brass at two, Jack,' he said. 'Have you finished that Adkin progress report?'

'Yessir. Got it done before I left last night. Anything new today?'

'Dora North is here.'

'Dora North? The cafe waitress, Pettifer's friend. Yes. You know, sir, I wouldn't be surprised if she's Dan North's sister. Remember Dan? They tell me he's going straight now.'

Hallam pressed his desk buzzer. 'We'll see what Dora has to say.'

Dora North was small, energetic, intense. Her dark hair, almost blue-black, her snapping brown eyes and her clean-cut features — there was a certain harsh beauty about her face — spoke of her gypsy blood.

Spratt put her into a chair, went back to his own desk and opened his notebook.

'Now, Miss North,' Hallam said pleasantly. 'You wish to speak to me?'

'If you're the person who's in charge of that case where the woman was killed — strangled — at Ashwood, I do. You see, I saw you and your pal here, from the caff, going in to Number Sixty-three, and I thought to myself, Cor, if they don't look like a couple of cops — policemen, I mean. Then later, when Mr. Herriot bobbed across for his usual pot and toasted teacake, I asked him if he had seen you. And when he said he had I said who were you after and he said you were putting the arm on him because you'd found out he was the chap who'd been robbing all these poor-boxes. Daft as a brush, Mr. Herriot is when he's that way out. So I said, No, honest, were they looking for Sid? And he said, well they did call at Sid's spot only he wasn't there and I said no well he wouldn't be.'

She broke off to unbutton her raincoat, beneath which, Hallam saw, she wore her waitress's uniform.

'Warm in here, isn't it?' she commented before she went on.

'Well, I thought it over and I was a bit worried, putting two and two together, like, so I slipped out to the 'Piper' yesterday and had a word with Mrs. Lister. She's a sweet woman, is Mrs. Lister. And she says, 'Well, Dora, if you've anything to say you must go and see Chief Inspector Hallam, who's in charge.' and she told me where to come. Which I did, last night, only you weren't here.'

Hallam had let her run on. He knew her type. She would have her say, would get a flood of unessential preliminaries off her chest before she reached the business in hand, and no power on earth could stop her.

'I see,' he said, 'And now, what have you to tell me?'

'Mister, I don't care what anybody says, Sid Pettifer didn't do that woman and don't you go thinking he did!'

'Why do you imagine we suspect him, Miss North?'

'Because Sid's staying up there just now and there's some around here who'll tell you he's got a quick temper, but it means nothing, doesn't that.'

'You and Mr. Pettifer are still friendly?'

'Of course we're friendly. Sid would never walk out on me, not for keeps. I mean, just now, living at her house like he is, well, it's not like it used to be, but as Sid says, that's only temp'ry and she can do him a lot of good, which I didn't understand at first and acted up with him, I must say.'

Hallam spoke casually. 'I can quite understand Mrs. Kaye is the sort of patient Mr. Pettifer could do with in his business.'

'Ooh, she is! I mean, well-off and lots of posh friends and that. Like a fool, I thought she and Sid were — well, you know, starting an affair. And Sid was wrong there, I mean, not telling me the true facts about her offering to help him, to bring his great talent before the world, like. I mean, if he'd said so, I'd never have gone up there that night to have it out with him and her face to face. Upset Sid, I did, going there like that. But I never stopped to think, you see. That's me all over, never stopping to think. But Sid'll come back to me, I know he will.' She seemed suddenly conscious of the desperate note which was shrilling her voice. She stopped, swallowing painfully. 'Like I said, mister, Sid wouldn't have anything to do with that murder job. I mean, it'd make a mess of everything for him, wouldn't it, and things going his way at last. So I thought I'd better come and tell you.'

'You're sure that's all you have to tell us?'

''Course it is. What else is there?'

'You seem to have put yourself to

considerable trouble to make sure Mr. Pettifer isn't accused, Miss North. Why should he be?'

'Well, he and me did have these rows about this woman. And I thought if somebody had heard us in that lane, or Mr. Walsh had said anything, because I saw him watching through his door which is just under Sid's place, and these rows were all my fault and not Sid's. I mean, I started them. Look, I've got to go now.'

'Of course, Miss North. Thank you for coming in. Just one more question. You've known Mr. Pettifer for quite some time?'

'Yes. Him and me — well, you know how it is. Nothing definite, like. Up to now Sid hasn't been the marrying kind. Gets his fun from women another way, I always tell him. Joking, of course,' she added hurriedly and rose quickly from her chair.

Spratt saw her out. He came back and closed the office door.

'What d'you think she meant by that last remark about Pettifer, sir? I expected you to take her up on it.'

'She didn't mean to say it, Jack. When

it slipped out, I saw her shut up like a vice. Waste of time trying to make her open up.' He began to fill his pipe. 'This damn Pettifer — we don't seem able to get him out of our hair.' He struck a match and puffed lustily. 'Look, I've an idea what Dora North was hinting at just now. It might pay to follow it up. Can you get me one of the women police here, Jack? Let's see . . . Ah, Jones. Tell her I've a job for her.'

Woman Police Constable Mary Jones was fair-haired and very attractive. She was slenderly built, almost fragile, yet she had been known to handle a couple of truculent drunks most competently without assistance, without turning one of those golden hairs, either.

Hallam briefed her quickly. 'I want you to fix up a treatment with this chap, Mary. I'd like to know what methods he uses, so you'll have to fake some complaint.'

'Fibrositis?' Mary suggested. 'My mother's a martyr to it, I know all the symptoms and there's nothing to show you haven't got it. Whereabouts do you think, sir?'

'I'd settle for the small of the back if I

were you. It's a common place. Tell him you have lumbago. Here's the number you ring.'

He gave her the Kayes' number in Granville Road. Spratt handed her his receiver, with an outside line already cleared for her.

At the ninth ring the call was answered. A woman's voice repeated the number. 'Mrs. Kaye here,' it added.

'Good morning,' Mary greeted. 'I want to speak to Mr. Pettifer, please.'

'Who is calling?'

Mary gave her name. 'I'm hoping he will be able to give me some treatment for lumbago.'

'I'm sorry.' Stella Kaye's voice was cold, definite. 'Mr. Pettifer isn't seeing any new patients at present.'

'Oh.' The policewoman covered the receiver and relayed the message to Hallam.

'Stick to it. Insist,' he said quickly. Mary took a deep breath.

'Hello? Look, I must see him, it's most important. He hasn't given up his practice, has he?'

'Not exactly. It's just that he is having a break — a rest — at present.'

'Could you tell me when he is likely to be back at work? Or how I could get in touch with him personally?'

The listeners heard an annoyed, impatient exclamation from the line.

'Oh, well — ! Perhaps you'd better talk to him. Hold on.'

Mary winked triumphantly at Spratt. Pettifer, breathing somewhat heavily, announced himself.

When she thought fit to use it, Mary Jones had a warm, seductive voice. The honeyed tones in which she pleaded for an appointment would have crumbled the Rock of Gibralter. She let Pettifer know she was young and unmarried, and he arranged to see her on Saturday morning, at his Dean Street room. She thanked him effusively and assured him she would be there on the dot.

'Is that all for now, sir?' she asked when she had replaced the receiver, and when Hallam said yes, she said she would go back to the Women's Department and practise groaning realistically.

Hallam shrugged and settled to his paper-work.

For over and hour he ploughed on, routine stuff, most of it, while Spratt went and came at intervals, busy with his own particular tasks. When Hallam finally signed the last report and flung it into his Out tray, Spratt was back at his desk, absorbedly reading.

'What's that you've got, Jack?' Hallam craned forward and answered his own question. 'Oh, Madge Adkin's diary. Any use?'

'There's just one thing, sir . . . She seems to have been a factual sort of writer. I mean, she didn't indulge in imaginative stuff, nor even comment. Every day she made a note of the weather, of any correspondence received or sent, and so on. No notes on bird life, by the way. It's just a plain straightforward record except for that one thing I mentioned. Every now and then, at the end of the day's events, she's put down a number.'

'A number,' Hallam repeated.

'Yes, sir. I've made a list — 4, 6, 10, 6,

20, 18, 26, 26. They appear in the diary in a very irregular manner. There are three clear days between the four and the first six, for instance, and eighteen days between that six and the next number, ten. Then comes the second six, the day after the ten, then a long interval, another long one, with two shorts to end with.' He looked up hopefully. 'Any ideas, sir?'

Hallam glanced through the list. 'To start with, they are all even numbers, as you'll have noticed. The range is from four to twenty-six. That suggest anything?'

'Could they be house numbers?'

'Let's suppose they are, Jack. Let's take it the numbers are those of houses in Granville Road. You say she put down all the events and visitors of each day. Maybe these are houses she herself visited.'

Spratt shook his head. 'Doesn't fit, sir. The diary mentions Mrs. and Miss Pelling at Number Twenty-one — you know, Madge's friend who works at the brewery offices. Madge used to have an afternoon cup of tea with them most Wednesdays. She mentions it in here.' He tapped the diary. 'She says nothing of paying other calls anywhere in the road.'

Hallam considered for some moments. Then he said, 'Go out to Granville Road, Jack. Find out which people on the even-numbers side have young children and keep dogs.'

Granville Road lay in mid-morning calm under a warm autumn sun when Spratt arrived. At the lower end of the road, James Tanner was cutting the outside grass of the end house, opposite the Kayes'. Spratt drew in beside him and got out of the car.

'Morning!' Tanner replied to his greeting and leant on the handles of his machine. 'There's one thing about winter — no blasted lawn mowing to do. Ah, you're the sergeant as was with Mr. Hallam in his office. How's things, then?'

'Going forward,' Spratt replied non-committally. 'Mr. Tanner, I think you could help me.'

'What, now? Look, I'm supposed to be at work.'

'It'll take less than a minute. Just two questions. First, could you tell me all the people on that side of the street' — he nodded — 'who have children?'

'Halls at Number Four, lad of ten, two boys in their teens next door — Furness's, that is,' Tanner replied promptly. 'Twins at Grayles, Number Ten, little lasses just started at a private school. Gowers at Fourteen have one lad, so do Brays at Eighteen. Next but one to them, young Christine Benton. Kayes, across the road yonder, have two young lads.' He squinted at Spratt's notebook. 'Got it all down?'

'Yes. Now, what about dogs, same side of the street?'

Tanner took a little time to reply.

'Now, then,' he said. 'Poodle at the top house, Browns. Gowers at Fourteen have a black and white mongrel. Next door to them is Wests, they have a Labrador. The only other dog is an old Scottie at Bentons, Number Twenty-two.'

Spratt closed his notebook. 'That's fine, Mr. Tanner. And thanks very much. Now go on, ask me what it's all about.'

'Nay, Sergeant. That's your business, not mine.' He spat on his hands and stepped away along the grass verge, behind the whirling blades.

11

Spratt walked across the C.I.D. office and laid a sheet of paper on his chief inspector's desk.

'This is the break-down, sir. As you see by the code signs I've made, there are seven houses with children, and four families keep dogs. In two cases there are both dogs and children.'

'Good. Now, the first thing I want is at least one house with a child or children and no dog. Let's see . . . Ah, five of them. Numbers Four, Six, Ten, Eighteen and Twenty-six. Now, these ticks represent numbers from the diary? Right. And we have four of them in the no-dog-but-children class. Good again.'

He looked up to meet his sergeant's disapproving gaze. Spratt was both offended and annoyed when Hallam had one of his mysterious I've-seen-it-so-should-you turns.

'One other thing, Jack. You've made a

note, I'm sure, of the dates under which the numbers appeared in the diary?'

'Yes, sir.'

'And the last one is — ?'

'Seventh of September. Last Friday. A week ago tomorrow.'

Hallam beamed. 'That's fine! That's just what we want — I hope. Now this is my idea. When Madge Adkin took her nightly walks, it wasn't bird life she was interested in, but her neighbours. I think she went down Gypsy Lane after dark to do a bit of spying on them. Remember, she led a dull life — she always had — and to a woman of that sort her neighbours are of intense interest, you know. It would be easy for her to get into anybody's garden at that side of the street, from Gypsy Lane. There are occasional gates and a gap or two, and most of the fences and walls between the gardens are low enough to be climbed by a long-legged, active woman. You'll note none of the numbers from the diary correspond with those of the houses where there are dogs. A dog might give the show away if he heard a prowler on his master's property.'

Spratt rubbed his chin doubtfully.

'I must say it sounds a bit far-fetched to me. Look, sir, she went out late at night, when most folks would be in bed. What would she see of them?'

Hallam spoke slowly, carefully. 'I think it possible she did more than try to spy. I think, when she found a chance, she entered people's houses. Not to steal or do damage. Probably just for kicks. And when she was successful in doing this, she carried away and kept, as a sort of trophy, some small and worthless object, which would probably never be missed.'

Spratt let out a long breath. 'I see. Those things on the mantelpiece in her bedroom. They've been worrying me a lot.' He took an envelope from his desk and emptied it out. 'Yes, here we are. Cigar stub, shirt button, paper clip, empty matchbox, tiddly-wink, twist of wool, sugar lump. Tiddley-wink,' he repeated. 'Now I know why you wanted details about children.'

'That's it. We're far from setting up any definite theory yet; we'll have to make a few more visits. You see — you didn't know this — that chap Pettifer thought he heard someone in the Kayes' garden one night. He put the occurrence at 'last Friday or Saturday.' There was a number noted in the diary on Friday.'

'And, by damn, that number was twenty-six, sir. The Kayes' house number. That comes twice in the list. Now — seven objects from the mantelpiece, eight numbers, two of them — six and twenty-six — twice. One — er — trophy short, sir.'

'That's not significant. It's possible she didn't always find one handy.' He glanced at his watch. 'We're about due at the A.C.C's office. Just time to make a list of names of owners of those house numbers. Can you do it?'

'In no time, sir. I have the preliminary house-to-house reports here. I'll get the details from them.'

Hallam nodded and turned to the notes he had made, weapons of aggression, and, he hoped, of defence also, in the coming interview. Philip Daly, the Assistant Chief Constable, liked swift progress and rapid results. Hallam was ruefully conscious that, at the moment, he had neither much progress to report nor a great deal of further action to suggest.

However, he had a staunch ally in Chief Superintendent Herbert Gale. The super was a grey-haired mountain of a man, who had come up the hard way, step by painfully-accomplished step. When, that afternoon, Hallam faced the slightly-built, granite-featured Daly across the A.C.C's desk, with Spratt in attendance, he was heartened to see Gale's quick, reassuring wink. He knew Herbert Gale was solidly behind him.

Having dealt swiftly and competently with a couple of routine matters, Daly made fists of his hands and set them together on the desk in front of him.

'And now,' he said, 'this Adkin case. Hallam, let's hear from you.'

'We're still at the inquiries stage, sir. We've turned up nothing yet to give us a definite lead. One slight possibility has suggested itself this morning. We propose to follow it up at once.'

'H'm.' Daly was not pleased. 'What about the escaped man, Mitchell? You don't consider him suspect?'

'We can find nothing against him at the moment, sir. I'm not saying he's definitely in the clear. At any rate, if we want him again, we know where to lay our hands on him.'

'I've read your reports, Hallam. They are woefully thin.'

Hallam had no reply to this. The Assistant Chief was right. And Hallam wasn't fool enough to offer any excuses.

'Complicated businesses, these suburban jobs are,' Gale said comfortably in his deep rumbling voice. 'Middle-class folk are too much like those three much-quoted monkeys.'

'That may be so, Chief Superintendent,' Daly said acidly. 'But the hard fact is that we have a suburban case which isn't broken yet. It's not even cracked. More than forty-eight hours gone, too.' He shrugged. 'The inquest tomorrow — we'll have to get it adjourned, of course.'

'Could have been worse, I suppose,'

Hallam commented to Spratt as they descended the stairs to C.I.D. 'Anyway, let's have a look at those names you listed.'

Spratt carried the file across to Hallam's desk as soon as the chief inspector was seated.

'Working from the top of the road, sir, we have Donald Hall first. Insurance agent. Wife, and daughter aged ten. Next on the list is William Furness, at Number Six. Big detached house, that. He's the proprietor of the Furness car showrooms in South Street. Plenty of money there, I'd say. I'll bet he smokes cigars, too. Which would account for that butt we found in the collection.'

'Hold on — let's not go too fast on the theory.' Hallam peered at the list. 'Number Ten, Grayle. Electrical Salesman — O'Donnel and Shawforth — I know their place. Wife and twin daughters, five year olds.'

'Furness has two lads also, sir. Early teens. They're away at boarding school. Then we get on to Number Eighteen, Bray. Departmental Manager at Silkin's.

Wife, boy of eleven. That leaves the Kaye family, sir.'

'And the Kaye family seems to crop up all over the place. Well, now. I'd like you to see the Halls, the Furnesses, the Grayles and the Brays. You know what you're after — you're trying to match up, as far as possible, that collection of objects with these four families. We'll visit the Kayes together. I'd like your impressions of that lot. If you get out there now you can clear it up this afternoon, and we'll call on the Kayes after tea, when — Come in!' He broke off to answer the knock on his office door. A duty constable stepped in smartly.

'A man named Benton wants to see the officer in charge of the Adkin case, sir. He's a resident of Granville Road and says he has important information. He has his young daughter with him.'

'I've met him, though he isn't aware of it,' Hallam replied. 'Right, I'll see them. You'd better hang on,' he told Spratt, who was reaching for his hat. 'Let's see what this chap has to say.'

The dumpy, bespectacled Benton came

bustling in, almost dragging a tall, dark-haired girl with him. He stopped so short on seeing Hallam that his daughter stumbled into his heels.

'Good afternoon, sir,' Hallam said pleasantly. 'I am Detective Chief Inspector Hallam. Detective Sergeant Spratt is helping me with the Adkin case. Please sit down, both of you.'

Benton seated himself fussily and with a certain amount of confusion.

'About last night, Chief Inspector. Of course, I had no idea then. If I expressed myself too forcibly, well . . . You might at least have said who you were.'

Hallam shrugged. 'You have some information for me, sir?'

'I certainly have.' Benton's aggressive bounce came back at once. 'This is my daughter Christine. This afternoon she had a most distressing experience. On Granville Common. Tell Mr. Hallam all about it, girl.'

She spoke in a mutter which verged on sullenness.

'I was walking on the Common. A man stopped me. He tried to — to interfere with me. I screamed and he ran away.'

'She came home in a dreadful state,' Benton interposed. 'Crying hysterically, hardly able to tell us. And no wonder, poor child. I was at home — I'm a research chemist at Barker's and Thursday is my half day. I got the car out and brought her down here. You've got to do something about it!'

'Will you give me a description of this man, please, Miss Benton?' Spratt asked quietly.

The girl — Hallam recognized her as the pupil whom Crane had dismissed — flushed uncomfortably. In contrast to her father, she was long and thin, all awkward angles and badly co-ordinated movements. Age about fifteen, Hallam guessed. She had a narrow, plain face and a small, peevish mouth. She shrugged helplessly.

'He was just ordinary looking,' she said.

'Ordinary looking,' Spratt repeated. 'Let's see if we can do a bit better than that. Was he tall or short?'

'Sort of medium. He wore dark glasses.'

'A young man?'

'No.' She paused for several moments. 'About daddy's age, I should say.'

'Well, now, what was he wearing?'

'He had a brownish kind of trilby hat pulled down over his face. And a mackintosh — a fawn-coloured one. That's all I noticed.'

'Have you ever seen him before?'

'No.' Again she paused and then, 'There was a car standing some distance away, on the sandy road which runs across the Common. A dark blue car. A small one. I think it might have belonged to this man. I mean, there was nobody else about.'

'Did you notice the make, or the number?'

'No. It was too far away.'

'Did you see him get out of this car?'

'No, but I've seen the car, or one like it, standing there before. In the evenings, when I've been taking the dog for a run on the Common.' Although her fingers were twisting ceaselessly in her lap, Christine Benton was speaking more clearly, more confidently now.

Hallam took up the questioning.

'Please tell us exactly what happened, from start to finish.'

The girl took a deep breath. 'I went for a walk on the Common after lunch. This man — well, he sort of appeared from behind one of the gorse bushes. He asked me if I could tell him the time and I looked at my watch and said it was a quarter to two. Then he stepped forward and flung his arms round me and — and he tried to kiss me.'

She stopped, flushing deeply. Her father gestured at her.

'Go on, Christine. Tell the whole story.'

Her lower lip went down. 'Must I, Daddy? I don't like.'

'Yes, you must. I know it's embarrassing, but these gentlemen won't mind. And they must be told.'

She gulped again. 'He tried to — to put his hand down my blouse. So I screamed, and he let me go and I ran home.'

'You didn't see where he went — whether he got into that car, or went towards it?'

'I didn't look round. I daren't. And I've

told you everything now.'

'You've told a nasty story very clearly,' Hallam said sympathetically. 'I'm sorry you had the experience, Christine. Have any of your friends run into the same sort of trouble on that Common, do you know?'

Her lank hair swung out as she shook her head.

'I see you are at the Girls' High School.' He nodded at the red and brown blazer she wore. 'You didn't go today?'

'Only this morning. We have a half-holiday.'

'I see. You say you usually walk on the Common in the evening? This afternoon was an exception?'

Colour flooded her face again. She glanced at her father.

'She rushed out of the house in rather a hurry, Chief Inspector,' he said. 'There had been a small and quite insignificant family tiff in connection with some riding lessons she had been having. Nothing of importance.'

Hallam nodded and turned to the girl again. 'You're sure you can't tell us anything else about this man? No? Well, look. We can't have this sort of thing going on, so we'll have to stop it. Don't worry any more about it, my dear.'

Benton had been silent too long. 'Of course you must stop it, Chief Inspector! I demand that. And, by the way, before we came here I made Christine go with me to the Common, to the exact spot where this maniac accosted her. No sign of him, or his car, by then, of course. I searched carefully around for clues, but there are none. At any rate, I've saved you the trouble of looking there.'

Hallam pushed back from his desk and got to his feet.

'I don't think we need keep you and the young lady any longer, sir. Thanks for coming along.'

'I have your word that the matter will be thoroughly investigated, and without delay?'

'You have, sir.' Hallam motioned towards the door which Spratt was holding open. Benton rose and followed his daughter out.

'Genuine, sir?' Spratt asked when they

were alone again.

'Could be. That Common's an ideal place for a queer to operate. You've been through the house-to-house reports. I take it there's no similar mention in them?'

'Not a single one, sir.'

'We'd better make dead certain, though. There's a post office and general shop on Ashwood Road, just past the doctor's surgery. Call in there while you're up doing those four houses. If there's been any gossip about odd men on the Common, the post office people'll be sure to have heard it. A place like that is the news centre of the district. Get off now, and I'll see you here again at six.'

'Very good, sir.' Spratt went out and Hallam returned to his desk. Christine Benton's story had put a new look on the Adkin case. If a sex maniac were operating in the Ashwood district, it was certainly conceivable he'd tangled with Madge Adkin. Such men weren't usually knocking about late at night, but there could be exceptions, of course.

Hallam moved irritably in his chair.

These creatures were the very devil to trap, but if there was one in the Ashwood region, trapped he must be . . . The old trick of using a policewoman for bait might not be dependable here. He made up his mind suddenly and left his office to walk along a corridor and up a flight of stairs to see Higgins, head of the Uniformed Branch.

As a result of his visit, P.C. Garrett, in plain clothes, knocked at Hallam's door later that afternoon and was told to come in and sit down.

'Garrett, I've a special job for you. You've been seconded to me for a few days. I'm giving you an assignment which I think a country-bred chap can do better than a townsman, and you fit the bill. I'll tell you all about it now so that you can think it over and work out your own plans. I want you on this job tomorrow.'

He told Garrett of Benton's visit, of Christine's story.

'I want an all-day watch kept on that Common,' he said, 'by a man who knows how to use cover and keep himself out of sight. Are you familiar with Granville Common?'

'No, sir. I've never been there.'

'Take a look.' Hallam spread out the large-scale map which lay on his desk. 'Here you are — Granville Road there, Gypsy Lane here. This, I would say, is the sandy road the girl mentioned, running across the Common. You'd better keep that in view as much as you can. You'll be in plain clothes, of course, and don't be disappointed if you draw blank. In view of his try on Christine Benton this afternoon, the fellow may lie low for a while. Everything clear?'

'If I should see this man, sir, do I bring him in?'

'Not unless he gets up to something. You'll note his car number, if he has a car. If not, stick to him till he goes to earth somewhere. Whatever happens, don't lose him.'

'I'll do my best, sir.' Garrett went off, obviously pleased with his orders. Hallam picked up the telephone and was put through to the Kayes.

Mrs. Kaye answered the call. In a

precise, neutral voice, she gave her number, but when Hallam announced himself, her tones came alive, warm and vibrant.

'Chief! How lovely of you to ring! I thought you'd forgotten me. And what can I do for you?'

Hallam said he would like to call that evening, between a quarter and half-past six, if this was convenient. 'Further inquiries, you know,' he added.

'Why, of course! That'll be fine — absolutely makes my day. 'Voir, then!'

As he put the receiver down, Hallam wondered what Jack Spratt would make of Stella Kaye.

12

It was ten minutes past six when Spratt reappeared at Headquarters, full of apologies. He had slipped home, when he had finished the Ashwood job, to look in on his elder son's birthday party, and had got caught in the rush-hour traffic on his return.

'It's all right, I'll hear your report in the car,' Hallam said. 'We'll take mine and you can spout forth as I drive.'

Spratt waited until they were clear of the town centre.

'Nothing from the post office about attacks on the Common,' he said then, bending his notebook open on his knee. 'In Granville Road I took the line that we had found one or two odd articles which might have some connection with Miss Adkin's death. The Halls at Number Four couldn't help me at all. A complete blank. Mrs. Furness, in the detached house next door, was very helpful, however. First, she told me her husband smoked a cigar every evening. We had two Number Sixes on our list, you remember, so I asked her what brand of matches she bought. The box we found in Miss Adkin's room was a Bluebell, and that's not a common brand in these parts. But Mrs. Furness always gets them — she deals with a supplier in town who happens to stock them.

'I went on to Number Eighteen — the Brays. They've a son of eleven who has a set of tiddly-winks and one was recently lost. A red one. That fits. But I had even better luck at Grayles, Number Ten. They have twins, five year old girls, and I saw them. They were wearing identical jerseys and the colour was the same as the twist of wool we found, a sort of medium rust. Mrs. Grayle had knitted the jerseys, I got her on talking about that job and she said she'd been lucky, estimating the amount of wool she needed. (I led her up to that, of course.) 'I finished the second one with just less than a yard to spare,' she said. And when I said that bit might come in handy for mending she said yes, but it seemed to have got itself mislaid. She couldn't find it anywhere.'

Hallam slowed for traffic lights, then swept forward as they changed in his favour.

'I shouldn't get too triumphant a note in your voice, Jack,' he warned. 'Madge could have picked up the cigar butt and the matchbox, and the wool, if she had that type of magpie mind, when she was paying a call at those houses.'

'Ah, but that's just what she never did, sir. I made a point of asking about that. The answer was the same at both places. They were good friends, in a neighbourly sort of way, with her but they never entered her house, nor did Madge visit them. And that's not all I found out.'

Hallam coughed gently. 'Carry on, Sergeant.'

'I noticed, sir, at the Brays, the Furnesses and the Grayles, obvious and easy means of illegal entry. At the Brays there's a landing window just above the flat roof of a shed, and this window is usually partly open for ventilation purposes. Furnesses have a Yale lock on the back door which you could slip back in a couple of seconds with a piece of celluloid, and no bolts. In one corner of the Grayles's lounge there's a small sash window simply asking to have its catch pushed back by a penknife blade.'

'Did you, as a good policeman, point these security deficiencies out to the householders?'

'Well, no, sir. I didn't want to start them thinking too much.'

Hallam negotiated a roundabout and headed for Ashwood Road.

'Madge Adkin had no celluloid on her when she was found, Jack. Nor a knife of any sort.'

'Maybe she was just doing a recce that night, sir.'

'In that case, why was she killed? Who is going to attack a person, especially a neighbour, found prowling round a house? Or even found actually inside? Imagine what would happen if a householder had heard her downstairs and caught her. 'Good God, it's Miss Adkin! What on earth — ?' And she stammers out some explanation, if she hasn't one all ready, just in case. She wouldn't likely start a fight, would she? No, we may be on the track of an explanation for her collection, but not on one for her death. I only wish we were.'

Spratt said, 'Aye,' glumly, and put his notebook away as Hallam turned into Granville Road.

Reginald Kaye opened the door of Number Twenty-six to them.

'Come in, both of you,' he said when Hallam had introduced his sergeant. 'My wife told me to expect you. She has had to go out, and she asked me to present her apologies. We'll go into the lounge — the two boys are playing Ludo in the dining-room. Keeps them quiet for a while. Sit down, gentlemen.'

Hallam settled himself on the settee, Spratt took one of the easy chairs. Kaye seated himself opposite the sergeant.

'Well, Chief Inspector, any progress on this sad case?'

'There is a line we're following up,' Hallam told him. 'That's chiefly why we're here. If Mr. Pettifer is still with you, perhaps we could see him, too?'

Kaye shrugged his heavy shoulders,

thrust out his short legs.

'He's out, too. Attending a — er — patient at his place of business in town. My wife ran him down there in the car.'

'Have you any idea when he'll be back, sir?'

'I'm afraid not. They said something about the possibility of being rather late home. That could mean — oh, ten, half-past — maybe even eleven.'

'Just the one patient, sir, I understood you to say?'

'I believe so.' Kaye's long, monkey-like arms were flung wide in an almost-helpless gesture. 'Is it necessary to check up on them like this?'

'Good gracious, sir, not at all. I was merely wondering if we should call again this evening, when they — Mr. Pettifer especially — would be here.'

Kaye's brows drew together. 'You're particularly interested in him?'

'We're interested in his story of a prowler outside here one night.'

'Yes, but he wasn't absolutely sure, you know.'

‘Nevertheless, I shall have to take him over the story again.’ Hallam leaned back against the settee cushions, his glance directly upon Kaye’s face. ‘Mr. Kaye, I think you should be told something, in strict confidence, of course.’

Kaye’s eyes widened, his hands came together in an interlocked finger-grip.

‘Whatever do you mean?’

‘I have your word that what I have to say will remain entirely with you?’

Kaye relaxed. ‘Of course, Hallam. Keeping confidences is a basic essential in my profession.’

Briefly, Hallam outlined the theory which Madge Adkin’s midnight journeys had suggested. ‘We feel she might have gone so far as to enter some of the houses round here, Mr. Kaye. We have a list she made of what may be house numbers on this side of the street, and yours — Twenty-six — appears on it twice.’

‘Odd sort of hobby,’ Kaye commented. ‘Still, she was of a certain age, as they say. But I don’t see how she could possibly have made an entry into this house. The front door is locked and bolted at night, and so is the kitchen door. I attend to those myself, without fail. As for the french windows here — take a look at them. I always see to their fastenings before I retire.'

Hallam nodded to Spratt who rose obediently. 'Nice secure job,' he reported after his inspection. 'Bolts top and bottom to guard both these glass doors, and a very strong lock which you can only free from inside.'

'Fair enough. And you've never found anything missing, not even a small article, Mr. Kaye?'

'As far as I know, never.'

'On the night of the death, Mrs. Kaye and Mr. Pettifer sat up after you had gone to bed. Was that just an isolated occurrence, or had they done so before?'

Kaye pursed his lips and frowned.

'It had become almost a custom.' His face cleared. 'You're wondering if one of them could have unbolted and unlocked these doors, perhaps to get a breath of fresh air before going to bed, and forgotten to refasten them? I can definitely say no to that. I'm a creature of habit, Hallam, and when I come down in the morning I invariably walk in here as soon as I have put the kettle on in the kitchen. I open these doors and step outside to take a look at the day. I should have noticed at once if they had ever been left undone.'

Hallam spread his palms. 'All this doesn't help our half-formed theory one little bit, Mr. Kaye.' He smiled ruefully. 'But we're used to that sort of thing. Well, that appears to be that. We won't take up any more of your time. Sorry Mr. Pettifer wasn't here. We'll have to see him again sometime.'

They were both on their feet, but Kaye showed no signs of rising to see them out. He seemed sunk in thought, biting his lower lip and frowning. Then he looked up at them.

'Before you go . . . . Please sit down again. There's something I feel I ought to discuss with you.'

Resolution was in his manner now, a little forced, perhaps, but none the less determined. The two policemen returned to their seats.

Kaye cleared his throat. 'I realize, in your investigations of this sad business, you will have talked to and questioned most of the people who live around here. You will have been interested in any — er — comments they may have made. I have no doubt that we have been the subject of some of those comments.'

Hallam answered cautiously.

'I'm afraid I can't discuss that, sir. Any information — or speculation — we've been given has been in confidence.'

'Which is as good as saying there has been gossip.' Kaye blew out his cheeks. 'I suppose it's only human nature. The unconventional is always suspect.'

There was a pause before he continued. 'The thing is this, my wife was nervously ill, and the orthodox medical profession seemed unable to do much for her. She heard of Sidney Pettifer and visited him for treatment. From the outset he helped her complaint enormously.

'She — we — were naturally grateful to Pettifer. We knew he was not making a very good living out of the work which is more of a vocation than a mere job to him. We felt the best return we could make was to help him all we could.'

'A very nice idea,' Hallam murmured.

'He was, at that time, visiting the house here to give my wife her treatments. She preferred this to going to Dean Street. To cut a long story short, we asked him to be our guest here for a while.

'Now' — he took another full breath — 'the point is this. Pettifer is a bit of a rough diamond. His speech and his manners are not those of the people who live in a district like this. Curiosity, no doubt, was aroused. Who was this man now living at Number Twenty-six, who never seemed to go to work, who spent the days alone in the house with Mrs. Kaye, who went out with her whenever she did?'

He paused and seemed to expect a comment.

'You, and Mrs. Kaye, I take it, have explained the situation, when you've had a chance, to your friends around here?' Hallam asked quietly.

'Well, no. We haven't lived here long, my wife has no women friends and I'm afraid

I'm not a very sociable type myself. I would say we are on good neighbourly terms with the people around, but not on intimate terms.'

He was silent for a considerable time, though it was obvious he had not yet finished.

'I had an anonymous letter recently, addressed to me at my office,' he said at last. 'The usual filth — that my wife was carrying on an affair with our guest, and why hadn't I the sense to stop it.'

'You destroyed this letter, Mr. Kaye? It's what people usually, and often mistakenly, do.'

'I showed it to my wife first. I felt it was only right to do so. She had a pretty definite idea who had sent it, and wanted to go across and tackle the person at once, but I dissuaded her. I pointed out she had no actual proof, that it would only cause further trouble and talk, and that the incident was best ignored. There have been no more letters and I trust you won't ask me who we suspected. I can tell you, however, that it was not Miss Adkin.'

'I'm glad you made that point, Mr.

Kaye,' Hallam said. He was in no hurry to go now. Kaye had given him a lead. 'I believe there was a little bit of trouble recently between Mr. Pettifer and a Miss Dora North?'

'Ah, yes. Quite a turmoil we had up here one evening. The girl, who, it seems, considered she had some claims on Pettifer's affections, turned up and was all set to make a fuss. It was clear she thought — she was absurdly mistaken, of course — that my wife was trying to cut her out! Eventually she calmed down, Pettifer took her outside and, I believe, gave her a good talking-to. And that was the end of it.' He frowned, as if a sudden thought had struck him. 'May I ask how you knew about the North girl, Hallam?'

'Her name happened to crop up,' Hallam said vaguely, but Kaye's frown did not clear. He drew breath to speak again, and at that moment the telephone in the hall began to ring and almost simultaneously there was a rush of sandalled feet from the dining-room next door.

'I'll get it, Daddy!' a boy's voice shouted.

They sat in silence while the young voice spoke twice, then the lounge door was swung open and a fair-haired lad, pulling himself up, said, ‘Excuse me, Daddy, but Mummy is on the phone and wants to speak to you.’

‘Thank you, Patrick.’ Kaye rose. ‘My apologies, gentlemen. Patrick will look after you till I come back.’

The boy closed the door behind his father and walked to the hearthrug. He stood on it, feet astride and hands clasped behind his back.

‘You’re detectives, aren’t you?’ he asked.

Hallam nodded. ‘Yes, Patrick.’ He put a hand behind him and from the back of one of the settee cushions he produced the cane which he had seen Mrs. Kaye push there on his previous visit. He began to bend it back and forth, idly. ‘I am Detective Chief Inspector Hallam, and this is my assistant, Detective Sergeant Spratt.’

‘I’m very pleased to meet you,’ Patrick said politely and then, quickly, ‘Where did you find that?’

'Isn't it yours, or your brother's? Or maybe it's one your mummy keeps if you aren't — you know.'

Another voice spoke from the opened door. A younger, smaller edition of Patrick Kaye stood there. 'It's Uncle Sid's cane. He hits mummy with it. But not becos she's naughty. She likes him to do it becos it makes her better. She told me so,' the boy went on, 'once when I was away from school with a sore throat and I went into the bedroom and mummy was lying on the bed and Uncle Sid was giving her a treatment. And he was — '

A pair of long arms seized the boy's shoulders, spun him round. 'Nearly bed-time, Gordon,' Reginald Kaye said. 'Your supper's in the kitchen, you can eat it there.'

'Yes, Daddy.' They both scampered off and Kaye, still in the doorway, looked from Hallam to Spratt.

'My wife.' He jerked his head backwards in the direction of the telephone. 'They've been delayed with this patient at Dean Street. They won't be leaving there for some considerable time.'

'Then we won't wait,' Hallam said. He dropped the cane on the settee. 'We'll see Mr. Pettifer later. I take it we can always find him here?'

Kaye's mouth set in a thin line. 'I suppose so,' he answered and moved to the hall to see them out.

Neither of them spoke until they were in the car and Hallam was driving up Granville Road. Then Spratt said, 'Out of the mouths of babes and sucklings . . . '

'Yes, Jack. The psychiatrists have a word for it. Sexual sadism, I think.'

'I know what you mean, sir. It's an aberration. The sort of thing where a man will pay a prostitute to cane him because he gets satisfaction that way. You remember Bella Crabthorne who used to work South Castle Street before she retired? She was telling me about it once. Seems it's not uncommon.'

'Though in this case, maybe, the man gets his pleasure from doing the beating?'

'Bella said she'd met one or two like that, too. Not that she'd ever go in for queers of any sort herself. Strictly conventional, Bella was. Looks like

Pettifer is one of those chaps, doesn't it?'

'Let's not do any jumping. We'll wait till Mary Jones reports on Saturday. It's getting late, but I'd like to pay one more call before we knock off.'

Spratt grinned. 'Dean Street, sir? To check that Pettifer and Mrs. Kaye aren't there?'

'We'll look rather a pair of idiots if they are,' Hallam chuckled.

But there was no light showing in the window of Pettifer's room when they parked across the street outside the 'Merry Piper'. They got out of the car, walked over to Sixty-three, and met Herriot, the commercial artist, on the front steps.

'Not wanting me, I hope?' he said pleasantly. 'I've got a hot date and I'm behind time now.'

'Not you, sir,' Hallam replied. 'We were going to call on Mr. Pettifer, if he's here.'

Herriot shook his head. 'You're unlucky. He hasn't been near his place tonight. I'm sure of it. I always hear him when he's around.'

'Thanks, you've saved us a climb,'

Hallam said. They stood aside to let Herriot pass them.

'Well, sir?' Spratt queried then.

'Not idiots after all, Jack. They went out tonight, deliberately, to avoid us. And that's not jumping to conclusions, either!'

13

The job Hallam had given him, to keep a watch on Granville Common, was one that appealed particularly to Richard Garrett. It was a break from routine; for once he would be operating as an individual and not as a puppet held on the string of a radio wave-length. And he was particularly interested in the Adkin case, since he had been in on it at the start.

He left Headquarters that Thursday afternoon determined to make what he could out of this. The patrol car which had brought him there had now gone back to its own occasions, as Garrett had expected. The big bugs were very careful, when they wanted to see you, to get you there in a hurry, but you had to find your own way back.

However, that suited him. He walked to the central bus station and took an Ashwood bus. He would have a run out to Granville Common now, to get the lie of the land. Pick a good O.P. now, and he could go directly to it tomorrow, instead of making himself conspicuous then by roaming all over the place in search of one.

Forty minutes later he was strolling gently across Granville Common. Apart from two women deep in conversation on a seat, each mechanically rocking a pram with one hand as they talked, and an elderly man walking an overfed spaniel, the place was deserted. Garrett had an excellent eye for country and he felt at home in a very few minutes.

Granville Common, he judged, occupied some thirty acres of heather and bracken, with the latter clearly ousting the former. There were bare patches of reddish sand here and there and a fair covering of gorse clumps, thickening towards one corner, where the land rose into a steepish little bluff. Garrett went towards this.

The bluff, on which half-a-dozen birch trees and one wind-swept thorn were growing, proved to be the top of a disused sand quarry which flattened out, below, to an overgrown track beside a pond. A line of posts and rails, reinforced by barbed wire, guarded the steep drop, and as he stood with his back to the rails, Garrett saw he had found an ideal observation post. The major part of the Common was within his view, including the sandy road which crossed it.

He squatted on his heels, then lay on his stomach, peering between two cushion-like clumps of heather. In either position the vision-range was good, and concealment for himself excellent.

He had already noted four moorhens and a pair of dabchicks on the pond below the quarry. Borrow his dad's binoculars and he was all set up here as a bird-watcher, if anyone came along and appeared curious.

He felt very satisfied with himself as he walked back across the Common to the bus terminus in Ashwood Road.

At ten o'clock the following morning he was in position. He had seen no living creature, except one scampering rabbit, on his way across the Common. He laid his plastic mac on the ground and put the small rucksack he carried beside it. For half an hour he stood with his back against one of the birches, alert and keen. An elderly man with a spaniel — the same couple he had seen on the previous afternoon — and a Land Rover which bumped along the sandy road from a neighbouring farm, Garrett guessed, were the sum total of his observations.

He sat down on his mac and took a newspaper from his rucksack. He read it with an eye constantly lifting to the scene ahead of him. The Land Rover danced its way homewards again, two dogs appeared in the distance, unaccompanied, and chased each other in circles for a while before they streaked away together. Time began to drag.

At half-past twelve he took out the sandwiches and flask of tea he had brought and ate and drank slowly, spinning the process out. The food and drink cheered him, banished the sense of futility which had been growing upon him. Watching and waiting, often for no results at all, was typical of police work.

And he was lucky — though the day was overcast it was quite pleasantly warm. He repacked his things in the rucksack and settled down again to his afternoon watch.

When he looked up it was to find the seat, the only one he had seen on the Common, occupied by a man. Garrett dropped prone, adjusted his binoculars and took a long, careful look at him. In no way did he represent the fellow Hallam had described. He was, Garrett thought, in his late forties, plumpish, prosperous-looking, very well dressed in a dark suit and a club tie. He was hatless, his hair was black but silvered over the ears. His tapping foot, his frequent glances at his wrist-watch and his constantly-turning head told Garrett the man was impatiently expecting another arrival.

A woman appeared from the direction of Granville Road. She was tall, fair-haired and wore a dark green dress and a wine-red cardigan. She carried a big black handbag under one arm. Garrett adjusted the focusing screw of his glasses. He nodded to himself. Yes, she was Mrs. Kaye, as he'd already guessed from her figure and colouring. The man on the seat stood up and waved her across to him.

Garrett grinned. Here was a meeting which could have nothing to do with the business on which he had been sent, but it was something interesting to watch, anyhow.

Mrs. Kaye joined the man on the seat. He began at once to talk eagerly, persuasively, to her. Mrs. Kaye, however, seemed unconcerned, almost uninterested. At last the man threw up his hands as if in helpless resignation. She leaned sideways then and laid a hand on his knee. She said something to him, they both got up and moved, out of Garrett's sight, into the depths of a clump of gorse some distance behind the seat. Garrett's soft wolf-whistle expressed his opinion of an obvious situation.

Conscientiously, since he was supposed to make a note of any significant happening that day, he entered the time and a brief report in his notebook. When he looked up again, a movement on the far side of the Common caught his eye. A figure was approaching stealthily, advancing, with some skill, from one patch of cover to the next.

Garrett snatched up his binoculars and bore them on the man. He began to breathe more quickly when the adjusting screw brought the newcomer clearly in focus. He wore a dark brown trilby low over his eyes, and a brown belted raincoat. Medium height. Garrett couldn't see, because of the hat brim, if he wore dark glasses. He was carrying something in one hand — yes, a camera.

He couldn't be on the accosting lark now, there were no children nor girls in sight. But, as he was moving very cautiously and nearing, with every careful step, the clump of bushes where the couple was, Garrett reckoned he could guess his aim. A Peeping Tom at the best; a blackmailer, with a candid photograph for evidence — and at a price — at the worst.

Garrett got to his knees and without taking his eyes off the man for more than a few seconds at a time, rapidly repacked his gear into the rucksack. He pulled the string tight, knotted it, strapped the bag and pushed it into a nearby clump of bracken. He had formed a plan. He would not show himself until the interloper had made his own play. If he took a shot, or a series of shots, from his camera at Mrs. Kaye and her pal, he would have committed an act likely to lead to a breach of the peace, at least. A good excuse, then, for Garrett to go out and say a few words.

The man in the raincoat was crouching now, inching forward. Garrett could see the curve of his shoulders, the crown of his brown felt hat. Garrett, too, began to move warily out into the open.

He heard the crack of the dead stick on which the man with the camera unwittingly trod, saw him jerk upright and raise his camera at the very instant as a startled, wrathful shout and a thin scream rang out from the gorse clump. Mrs. Kaye's companion sprang to his feet, but the other man turned with the speed of a striking snake, breaking into a fast-accelerating sprint away across the Common.

Garrett stopped moving. He had been brought up in hunting country and he knew the wisdom of not being in too big a hurry at the outset of a run. When a fox broke covert it paid to watch his line for a few seconds before laying hounds on. Garrett, at this moment both huntsman and pack, viewed the flying man's direction and picked a line of his own which should allow him to cut in neatly. Then he, too, bent his elbows and began to run.

He was not aware of the steep-sided ravine towards which his quarry was making. He had not explored so far the previous afternoon. The man disappeared suddenly from view, but he was still holding his original direction. Garrett raced on, and then, abruptly, pulled up. The sandy, crumbling sides of the ravine had appeared almost at his feet. He saw his man again, making good speed forward along the hollow ground.

The ravine bent away right-handed. Quickly, Garrett decided it would pay him to get down to the bottom of it, rather than to run along the top edge. He scrambled down as best he could and took up the chase again. The man was out of sight now, concealed by the bend. Garrett put on speed towards it. The ground rose sharply, became level. He found himself on the outskirts of Ash Wood, with not a soul in sight.

He halted to listen. He could hear no sound of footsteps in the wood. The trees grew thickly together with tall bracken between them. To beat such a wood for a fugitive who probably knew every square yard of the place by heart was a mere waste of time and effort. Lost him, Garrett thought glumly as he turned away.

He hurried back to the seat, but Mrs. Kaye and her friend had gone. That didn't matter. The main thing was, he'd made a mess of his assignment, had let the man slip through his fingers. Gloomily, he collected his rucksack. No use hanging about any longer now. His watch told him it was ten minutes to three.

At three o'clock he was in the public telephone box in Ashwood Road, ringing Headquarters. He was put through to

Hallam, who, with Spratt, had just returned from the adjourned inquest. In depressed tones though without self-excuses, Garrett made his report.

'A pity, but it can't be helped,' Hallam commented. 'You had bad luck, that was all. But it's quite possible Mrs. Kaye and her companion recognized this man, or, at least, can give us a good description of him. Hang on there, Garrett. I'm sending Sergeant Spratt up. Meet him at the top of Granville Road.'

Garrett stepped out of the box, greatly relieved. It seemed to be true what they said of Chief Inspector Hallam — he made every allowance, at any rate, once.

But when, some twenty minutes later, Spratt's car drew up and Garrett, on being motioned inside, said ruefully, 'Well, I made a right mess of the job, Sarge,' he received a grim nod.

'You did that, lad. We'll have to see if we can pick up the pieces now. Let's hope we can.'

Mrs. Kaye answered Spratt's ring. She was wearing the same outfit Garrett had seen on the Common, with the exception of the cardigan. Her large blue eyes opened widely as Spratt held out his warrant card and introduced himself.

'Come in!' she invited. She touched Garrett on the shoulder as he passed her. 'We've met before, haven't we? The other morning. You absolutely refused my offer of coffee. Come along, both of you. We'll go into the lounge.'

Pettifer was there, sprawling on the settee in an unbuttoned shirt which displayed the gingery hairs on his chest. He scowled up at them.

'You lot again? Wanting to see me, I suppose?'

'No, sir, not now.' Spratt took the chair Mrs. Kaye offered, and turned to her. 'We're making a rather private inquiry, madam. We would like to speak with you alone.'

Pettifer frowned, but made no attempt to move.

'Now, Sid,' Stella Kaye chided gently. 'You heard what the man said. Go and have a walk round the garden, or cut some bread for the children's tea, or something.'

'Oh, all right!' He lumbered to his feet. They heard him pound his way upstairs; a bedroom door slammed. Stella Kaye put on a bright, hostessy smile.

'You haven't brought my friend Chief with you this time?'

'Chief, madam?'

'Oh, Sergeant, not 'madam' all the time, please! My name's Stella. And I meant Mr. Hallam. 'Chief' is my pet name for him.'

She perched herself in her favourite attitude on an arm of the settee. 'Now,' she said, 'what is all this about? Chief was here last night, but unfortunately I had to go out. Is it because of that?'

'No, Mrs. Kaye. You were on the Common this afternoon?'

'Oh, yes. I often take a stroll there after lunch — a breath of fresh air, you know.'

'You met a friend there, a man. While you were with him, another man appeared and, I believe, tried to take a photograph of you.'

Watching, Garrett saw Spratt's words had rocked her, right back on her heels. Colour drained from her face and her nails dug into her dress at the knee.

'How on earth did you know . . .?' She swallowed and tried to relax. 'Of course! The constable here. He was on the Common, too. He chased this man.' She looked directly at Garrett. 'Did you catch him?'

'No, madam.'

'What were you doing there, anyway?'

Garrett's glance towards Spratt received a nod of assent.

'I was keeping observation for a man who assaulted a young girl there yesterday. We thought he might turn up again today.'

'And did he?'

'The man who sneaked up on you, madam, resembled the description we have.'

'But that's impossible! I mean . . .' She didn't say what she meant.

'Yes, Mrs. Kaye?' Spratt prodded.

'Well, it all sounds so ridiculous. I mean, people assaulting girls in a district like this. Doesn't it — to you?'

'That's as may be,' Spratt returned. 'Now, Mrs. Kaye, did you recognize the man who interrupted you and your friend?'

'No. No, I didn't.' The denial jerked out of her.

'You'd never seen him before?' She shook her head.

'Was he wearing dark glasses? Constable Garrett wasn't near enough to be sure of that.'

She shifted restlessly. 'I don't know what he was wearing. I can't describe him at all. I looked up, he was there, and then he was gone. I didn't get any sort of a look at him.'

'Maybe your companion did. Would you be good enough to tell us who he was?'

Now her face flamed scarlet.

'If you want to know — find out.'

Spratt shrugged. 'Very well, Mrs. Kaye. That shouldn't be difficult. Constable Garrett has a good description of him.'

'He's a local man,' Garrett added. 'He didn't arrive in a car, he hadn't walked far, either. His shoes said as much. And I've seen him somewhere around here before today.'

'All right, since you're so clever,' the woman said spitefully. 'It was Walter Newton — he lives up the street. Number Eleven, I believe. But it wasn't at all what you're thinking. I mean, I just happened to see him on the Common when I was out walking. He's a neighbour, so we had a chat.'

'Among the gorse bushes,' Garrett murmured and she turned on him like a spitting cat.

'Why the bloody hell can't you mind your own blasted business, you young sneak?' She sprang up and rushed to the door, flinging it open. 'Get the hell — Oh!'

Pettifer, in his stockinged feet, was tiptoeing away along the hall.

There was a sudden confused explosion — of Stella Kaye screaming abuse at Pettifer, of Pettifer shouting back at her. In the midst of it, Spratt led Garrett quietly away. They stepped out on to the front porch, and Spratt closed the door softly upon the tumult.

'Crimes of Paris!' he said. 'You expect that sort of thing in the dock area, but in the Ashwood district . . . Ah, well! They'll settle down and then she'll ring this Newton chap and warn him to have a good yarn ready for us. That can't be helped.'

'Newton!' Garrett said. 'I've got him now. Vaisey and Newton, the estate agents in Ford Row. He's putting up for councillor in this district at the next election.'

'Number Eleven, she 'said,' Spratt commented. 'Nip on ahead and see if he's at home.'

But the middle-aged maid who answered the door told Garrett her master would be at the office. She looked as if she thought that anyone who expected to find a working man at home at that hour of the day needed urgent mental treatment.

14

Spratt dismissed Garrett at Headquarters, telling him to ring in the following morning for further instructions, and went in to report to Hallam.

'You know, sir,' he concluded, 'I can't see this having anything to do with Madge Adkin's death. In fact, Pettifer and Mrs. Kaye seem to be getting into our hair to no purpose at all.'

'We'll have to do a bit of following-up, though,' Hallam replied, 'in view of the Benton girl's complaint. Newton may have recognized the snooper so it's Newton for us. On the other hand, it may be possible the Kaye woman recognized him, too, but doesn't want to admit it.'

'In which case,' Spratt added, 'she's probably got in touch with Newton at his office by now, and if he's in the same mind, we're handicapped at the start.'

Hallam got up from his desk. 'You're probably right but we've got to try it.

Vaisey and Newton in Ford Row. 'Tisn't far. We'll walk it.'

The estate agents' office was on the ground floor of a handsome modern building called Tremayne House. They walked up a flight of steps and into an office where two clerks, a man and a woman, were typing busily. A second man was speaking into a desk telephone, reassuring the person on the other end of the line that a buyer for his property would be found almost immediately. He was using the bright, confident house agent's voice which will not admit there can be any snags or difficulties in the world of real estate.

None of the three took the slightest notice of the two men who had halted at that point in the long counter which bore a notice 'Inquiries,' and Hallam had to cough twice before the man at the telephone covered his mouthpiece and yelled 'Beck!' at the pitch of his lungs.

A door at the rear opened and an ancient in a porter's uniform of dark green shuffled in.

'No,' he mumbled when Hallam put his

request, 'you can't see Mr. Newton, nor yet Mr. Vaisey, not wivout an appointment. Mr. Backhouse, yes. He's the junior partner. But not Mr. Newton nor yet Mr. Vaisey.'

'Mr. Newton is here now?' Hallam asked.

'He might be, for all I know. But you can't — '

Hallam nodded to Spratt, who flashed his warrant card. The old man bent to peer at it.

'Oh, police, eh? Whyn't you say so? Half a minute, then.'

He tottered to a wall telephone and spoke into it.

'He'll see you now,' he said when he returned. 'This way.' He opened a flap in the counter, preceded them along a passage and, at the foot of some stairs, pointed upwards. 'Left at the top, first door,' he muttered. 'I'd take you up meself only the doctor says I've got to watch stairs.'

'Walter Newton' was painted in black on the door's frosted-glass panel. Spratt knocked. They were bidden to enter.

Newton, dark, well-built, with a small black moustache which added distinction to an intelligent face, rose from behind a large handsome desk to greet them and to indicate chairs.

'Now, gentlemen, how can I help you?' he asked pleasantly.

Hallam went straight to the attack.

'I believe you know a Mrs. Kaye, of Granville Road, sir. Have you had any communication with her this afternoon?'

Newton leaned easily back in his chair, his hands falling, relaxed, into his lap. He looked across at his visitors, smiling faintly, with a touch of amusement. It struck Hallam that the man had rehearsed this pose. It was far too languid to be quite natural.

'As a matter of fact, Chief Inspector, I have. We met on Granville Common by appointment at two-thirty today, to discuss a business matter.'

'Rather an unusual venue for business, sir?'

Newton's smile was still pleasant. 'You may think so, if you wish.'

'And during the course of this business discussion, I believe a man took, or attempted to take, a photograph of Mrs. Kaye and yourself?'

'That is perfectly correct.'

'What was his motive, sir?'

Newton shrugged. 'He didn't stay long enough to tell us. He ran away, and was chased by a young man who turned up from somewhere near by.'

'If he took this photograph, sir, would it be for purposes of blackmail, do you imagine?'

Newton made a play of considering this. He frowned, leaned forward to put his elbows on his desk, to lace his fingers under his chin.

'Could be,' he said at last. 'But I should hardly imagine the results of the photograph would be of much value. Mrs. Kaye and I were hardly in a compromising position.' He dropped his hands and smiled broadly. 'I mean,' he added, 'I'm not going to charge the fellow unless he does try to get money from me.'

'So you know who he was, sir?'

'Why, of course. Chap called West. Colin West. He lives at Sixteen, Granville Road. He's a professional photographer.'

'You can swear to that, sir — the man who interrupted you was this Colin West?'

'In any Court you please, Chief Inspector. Though I still can't see — Ah!' His face lit up again as if he were animated by a suddenly-born idea. 'I think I have it! I am the prospective Conservative candidate at the next municipal elections in the Glenford and Ashwood Ward. West, I know, is a red-hot Socialist, out on the tip of the Left Wing. He may have thought, by taking what he hoped would be a damaging picture of me, to use it as anti-Tory propaganda.' He nodded, and went on. 'Yes, that was surely it. He crept up with his camera at the ready and took a quick snapshot, hoping for the best. He must have been woefully disappointed!'

'I'm glad he was, sir. Though, if I may say so, it might have been wiser to have had your business discussion in the open.'

He would not have been surprised if Newton had taken offence at the remark, but the estate agent merely shrugged.

'You're absolutely right, Chief Inspector. But you know how unreasonable women are. I had no desire to sit beneath a prickly gorse bush, but the seat on the Common wasn't to Mrs. Kaye's liking. There's one of the cross-rails missing, so, as she had a plastic mac in her handbag, she suggested we put it on the ground and use it instead of the seat.' He spread his hands. 'Quite satisfied now?'

'Yes, sir, and thank you for being so co-operative. We'll be on our way and let you get back to work.'

But Newton insisted on seeing them out personally. He ushered them to the front steps and waited there while they walked away. Hallam said to Spratt, 'Well?' and Spratt replied, 'Aye,' slowly and thoughtfully. He added, as they turned into police headquarters, 'What about West, sir? Do we tackle him now?'

'Yes, I think so. You nip along up there and do that job. If he could be the man we want for the Christine Benton business, bring him in for questioning.'

At Number Sixteen, Granville Road, Spratt's summons was answered by a thin, angular woman in her early forties. She had dusty brown hair, an anxious expression and a sharp-nosed ferrety face of such extreme plainness that Spratt instinctively glanced at the left hand she put up to her mouth on seeing him and found, as he had expected, that she wore no ring.

'City police, madam,' he said. 'Detective Sergeant Spratt. I would like a word with Mr. Colin West if he is at home.'

'Well, yes, he is,' she replied. 'I'll go and find him.' She half-turned away and then, 'Oh, perhaps you'd better come in and wait.'

She left Spratt standing in a narrow hall, and presently there came the stamping of gardening boots beyond the door which the woman had closed behind her, and a deep male voice answering her. The door opened and a man came towards Spratt. He was of medium height, with a shock of untidy fair hair, a long nose and a wide mouth which grinned expansively to show an excellent set of teeth. He wore a tartan shirt, old flannels and tennis shoes, the last clearly just put on.

'Hullo!' he said. 'What happened? Did

Newton squeak, or was it the fascinating Mrs. Kaye? Well, Sergeant, I know I shouldn't have done it. Something came over me — isn't that what they say? But it was fun while it lasted.'

'Would you care to tell me all about it here, sir, or would you prefer to make a statement at Headquarters?'

West's brow creased. 'Is it as serious as that? Look' — he opened a door — 'let's go into the dining-room. My sister has a friend in the lounge, having a cup of tea. Perhaps you'd like one yourself?'

Spratt refused the invitation and took the chair West indicated. The fair-haired man switched on an electric fire which stood in the hearth.

'Might as well be comfortable. Right. Where do you want me to start?'

'If you'd go over the events of this afternoon, sir . . . '

'Well, now. I'm a free-lance photographer. I do work for commercial firms, magazines — you'll know the sort of thing. This morning I finished off a job I was doing for a friend who writes do-it-yourself stuff for the magazines. I see to the necessary illustrations. I had lunch at his house, came home, stopped on the front path here to dead-head some dahlias. As I was doing so I saw Stella Kaye come out of her house, give a furtive sort of look around and go off in the direction of the Common. Knowing Stella, I was curious and I dogged after her. I saw her meet Newton and they went to ground in some gorse bushes. I still had my camera with me so I sneaked up, took a photograph and dodged away. And then some young chap appeared from nowhere and chased me. I had some difficulty in shaking him off. I came home, put the film in the developer — my friend wants the prints for his article in a hurry — changed and went out into the garden. I was there when you arrived.'

'And what was your object in taking the photograph, sir?'

West grinned. 'Ah, well, that's quite a long story, Sergeant. Want to hear it?'

'If you please, sir.'

'Right. Then, first of all, do you happen to know Mrs. Kaye?'

'I have met her once, sir.'

'Have you, now? Oh, boy!' He rolled his eyes upwards.

Spratt cocked his head sideways, but made no reply.

'Well, when the Kayes came to live here, they bought their house through Newton's firm. And, as I read it, Stella Kaye made a play for Walter Newton and he fell for it. He's married, but they all come alike to Stella. I don't know how far or for how long the business went, mind you, but I'd say, judging from subsequent events, and knowing that type of woman, it lasted just long enough on Stella's part for her to feel the need for a fresh bit of man, and that wouldn't be long. She picked on me as the next victim.'

With an excellent sense of timing he broke off to light a cigarette.

'We're neighbours, you see, and I'm often around. Actually, I first met her through Newton. I'd done some work for his firm, Stella wanted some good colour pictures of the house and garden to send to relatives, and Newton put her in touch with me. She soon let me know that if I was in the market for a nice cosy little affair, that was swell with her. But I'm not the type who hangs around married women, yet when I made this clear to Stella she became really keen. Wasn't used to rebuffs, I suppose.

'Newton got to know all about it — I'll bet it tickled her to tell him all about her new man — me. She was never off my neck, and Newton didn't like it. I suppose he looked on me as a rival — he needn't have worried! — for he saw to it his firm didn't give me any more work. That was a filthy trick and I was naturally sore.

'However, Stella suddenly began to ease off me, and then this scruffy-looking chap appeared — the one who is living there now. I was thankful to be free of her attentions, and, as I say, it was only sheer curiosity which made me follow her this afternoon. She looked as if she had an assignation and as, for once, the red-headed chap wasn't glued to her side, I wondered if he'd had his come-uppance and who was the latest mouthful. When I saw she was meeting Newton, I thought I'd get a bit of my own back by throwing a scare into him. He's going into local government work, you see, and he'd just hate the idea I had something I could use against him. Of course, I wouldn't have done. Just a minute — I'll show you the negative. It's rather fancy — Stella at her best.'

He was off before Spratt could either agree or decline. The thud of his feet on the stairs was continued across the floor above. Then, after a pause, the sounds were reversed and West reappeared, grinning and shaking drops of moisture from the piece of film he carried.

'Here, hold it up to the light. It's quite a sharp image.'

Spratt did so. The negative showed a man and a woman framed by the stiff, untidy outlines of gorse branches. He was kneeling up, facing the camera. Mrs. Kaye was sitting, supported by her hands on each side of her. Her feet were spread apart and the skirt of her dress was up well above her knees. Beneath it, the camera had recorded a glimpse of the curving undersides of her generously-made thighs.

Spratt primmed his lips and handed the negative back.

'Proper cheesecake, eh?' the photographer commented. 'Cut him out, blow her up nicely and I've a pic I could sell to more than one periodical. But I don't deal in that line of business.' He stuffed the negative carelessly into a pocket of his flannels and sat down. 'Now, what next?'

'The main reason for my visit this afternoon is to discuss a far more serious matter than the photograph with you, sir.'

'Ah!' West nodded solemnly. 'Poor Miss Adkin! But I'm sorry, I can't tell you any more than I did the policeman who was here on the day of her death. Nor can Florence, my sister. We weren't able to help at all.'

'Oh, it's not that, sir. Do you mind telling me where you were and what you did yesterday afternoon?'

'Why, sure. I had lunch at home at a quarter to one, left the house to catch the one-thirty bus, since my car's in dock at the moment. Had a stroke of luck, though. Furness, the car salesman who lives up the road, was just backing out of his drive as I went by. He called out was I going to town and when I said I was he told me to get in, he'd give me a lift. I took a bus from City Centre to Trafalgar Road, to Cawson's engineering works. They're bringing out a brochure to mark their centenary and I've done the illustrations for it. I had the negs and prints with me and I spent over an hour in John Cawson's office, discussing them with him and his P.R.O. The said P.R.O. then took me down to the works canteen for a cup of tea. I left there about four, did some shopping in town, arrived home five-twenty. How's that? Okay? Now tell me why.'

'You weren't on Granville Common at all yesterday afternoon?'

'Definitely no.'

'And, of course, the people you've mentioned would swear to your presence with them at the stated times?'

'Unless they were the most confounded bloody liars, and I've no reason to think any of them are. Come on, what's all this about?'

'Well, don't take it the wrong way, sir.

We had a complaint made yesterday that a man had assaulted a young girl on the Common. The girl gave a description, rather vague, but enough to work on. We had a man planted there today, watching the Common. Your build and dress suggested to him you might be the fellow we wanted. When he saw you acting in a rather suspicious manner, he felt he had something to go on. He was the one who chased you. We had to find out who you were — our man had recognized Mrs. Kaye. Our questioning of her led me to you. Please realize I'm giving you these facts in confidence, sir. You've been very co-operative with me, and I feel it only fair to return the compliment.'

'I won't run off at the mouth, Sergeant. And as for the idea of my assaulting young girls, that's way out. I'm not any sort of a queer and if I want sex I get it in a normal way. I hope you find this skunk. I've a very sharp knife in my workroom, I use it for trimming prints. I'd like to doctor him with it, like they do male cats.'

'Aye.' Spratt nodded. 'They could do

with it, that sort. Well, I'll be getting on, sir, and thanks.'

'Right. And you can depend on me to keep my mouth shut. As for this' — he produced the negative again — 'it's going into the kitchen fire. I've had my fun with it.'

'That's probably the best place for it, Mr. West.' Spratt bade him good-day and drove thoughtfully back to town.

15

W.P.C. Mary Jones wore plainclothes for her appointment with Sidney Pettifer. She took the staircase at the Dean Street building two steps at a time and arrived outside Pettifer's door with her breathing still regular. She patted her fair hair before she knocked and received an invitation to 'Come right in.'

Pettifer was leaning against a small table with his back to the window, but there was enough light for Mary to mark the appreciative lift of his eyebrows at her appearance. She hoped he wasn't going to be difficult. She'd never tackled a man when she was undressed.

The sweep of her glance around the room showed her a dusty, uncared-for place. There was a treatment couch in the centre with a felt pad on it, anatomical charts on the grimy, colour-washed walls, and a screen in one corner. A plaster-board partition cut off one end of the room. Here, she guessed, were the sleeping quarters. The wooden floor, splintered in places, called out for a sweeping brush and the window was fouled with cobwebs at its corners. The place smelt stale, there was a general unaired mustiness there, sharpened by the cigarette Pettifer held between yellowed fingers.

'Miss Jones,' she announced herself. 'I have an appointment.'

'That's right, luv.' He was still eyeing her steadily. 'Sit down on the couch yonder and tell me what ails yer, then. Half a minute, though. Let's get the details down.'

He reached out behind him, lifted a grubby-looking ledger from the table and opened it, one-handed, at a place marked by an inserted ball-point pen. He stuck the cigarette in his mouth and spoke round it.

'Nah, what's yer first name?'

'Mary.' He wrote it down. 'Address?' She gave her private one. 'Age? And occupation?'

'I'm twenty-three and I work in an office.'

'And what did you say yer trouble was, luv?'

Graphically, with her hands on the small of her back, Mary described the throes of lumbago. Then, recollecting how briskly she had walked upstairs and into the room — that had been a mistake — she added it was much better this morning, but she had a distinct feeling it might come on again any minute.

Pettifer nodded and put his ledger down.

'Nah, look,' he said. 'Most complaints folks come 'ere to see me about is due to one thing and one thing only. That's what we call tension. You gotta learn to relax to start getting rid of it, see? You gotta relax yer mind as well as yer body. So I call you Mary and you call me Sid. That way, there's a friendly atmosphere, like, and that helps this 'ere relaxation I bin telling yer about. Okay?'

Mary looked up at him from beneath long lashes.

'Yes, Sid.'

'Swell.' He pushed away from the table, went to a wall cupboard and took out a large garment in blue flannel which he handed to her.

'You undress behind the screen. Take off that coat and skirt, yer blouse and anything else you got under it. You can keep yer bra and panties on, but you won't want shoes nor stockings. Get into this robe and I'll have a go at yer.'

Mary picked up the robe and retreated. Behind the screen there was another small table, a wooden chair and a clothes hook plugged into the wall. She undressed as Pettifer had directed her. The robe he had given her was not too clean, she found it was free at the back with no front opening. There were sleeves through which she thrust her bare arms, shuddering distastefully and promising herself a bath as soon as she returned home.

She found two large buttons, with loops to contain them, at the top and waist of the open-backed garment. Having fastened these she stepped out into the middle of the room.

'Right, pet,' Pettifer said. 'Lay down on the couch yonder, face down.'

Remembering her act now, Mary mounted the couch awkwardly rolling over with a half-stifled groan. Pettifer took off his jacket and rolled up his shirt sleeves, exposing powerful forearms which glinted with golden-red hairs.

'Nah,' he said. 'I want yer to relax completely. Drop them arms loose, like you was dropping them on the floor. You gotta let every bit of yerself go, like. Just as if you was an empty sack lying there. Go on, let go. More. More still. Much as yer can. You done it? You're completely relaxed, like I said? Right. Keep it that way.'

He put his hands in under the robe and began to massage her back with long sweeping strokes, his thumbs running down the line of her spine.

Ten minutes later he straightened up. 'Right, luv,' he said again. 'Now we got the trouble where we want it. Concentrated, all of it, between here and here.' He put one hand on the small of her back, the other across the tops of her thighs. 'Now comes the time when we has to break it up, tap it away.'

He tapped her buttocks lightly. 'Here's where I've got it now. And here's where it's going to go from.' The tapping, with all the fingers of both his hands, became quicker, deeper. Mary wasn't sure she liked this but she thought if she objected now she would look rather foolish. Pettifer was there to give her treatment, she had asked for it and if these were his methods she couldn't very well disapprove as long as he didn't . . .

Now came a change. He was striking at her with the edges of his palms. It didn't hurt, in fact, it was mildly pleasant. But it seemed to be taking something out of Pettifer. She could hear his breathing quicken and become almost hoarse.

The hacking ceased. Now he was smacking at her, with the flat of each hand alternately. And he was beginning to hurt her.

'Ooh!' she said, and tried to keep her tone light. 'That's murderous. I can't stand any more.'

She swung her legs sideways and rolled, to come upright with her feet on the floor. But she had only begun the movement when the door was flung open. A woman's voice shouted, 'Sid! Stop it

— do you hear — stop it!'

On her feet now, Mary turned to see a tall, well-made, well-dressed blonde woman standing there, her blue eyes furious, her face a hideous mask of rage. Pettifer was staring at her like a sleep-walker violently awakened. He was still breathing hard, and his face shone with sweat. He opened his mouth and managed to say, 'Stella! What you doing 'ere?'

Pulling her robe together behind her, Mary sat quietly down on the edge of the massage couch. This, she felt, might prove very interesting.

The other woman came into the room, closing the door behind her. The hard lines of her face smoothed themselves out and she gave Mary a token smile.

'Hallo,' she said. 'I'm Stella Kaye.' She turned towards Pettifer. 'I got through my shopping in town quicker than I expected, Sid. So I thought I'd drop by and run you home.' Then she looked at Mary again. 'Sorry about the dramatic entry, but Sid does get carried away by his healing enthusiasm at times. I could see at once he had given you enough treatment, as much as you could stand. I'm sure you agree?'

'It was getting a little severe,' Mary admitted.

'Well, Miss — er — Your treatment is over. You can get dressed.'

'Thank you very much, I'm sure,' Mary replied demurely. She smiled warmly at Pettifer, who snatched the half-smoked cigarette from behind his ear, lit it shakily and began to gulp smoke. Without hurrying, Mary retreated behind the screen. She dressed, her ears straining to catch the import of a whispered conversation during which Stella Kaye's sibilants hissed snake-like and the answering murmurs of Pettifer seemed to be propitiatory. But the words, on both sides, were indistinct.

When Mary emerged, with her purse at the ready, Stella Kaye was leaning against the table which held the ledger, and Mary sensed a sharpening of the older woman's dislike for her. Mary knew why. She was looking her best again now, with all her clothes and fresh makeup on. Stella Kaye was seeing her as she was, young, attractive, full of vitality. And no doubt she was doing a bit of self-comparison.

'Now, Sid,' Mary said brightly. 'How much do I owe you?'

'Half a — ' he began, but Mrs. Kaye cut in like a knife slash.

'Two guineas, Miss — er — '

'And well worth it,' Mary returned pleasantly, hoping the Expenses Department wouldn't baulk at paying four times a normal charge. 'I feel a million, thanks to you, Sid.'

She laid two pound notes on the massage couch and began to search for a florin. Pettifer began again.

'Look here, I don't usually — ' but Mrs. Kaye cut him off for the second time.

'If you haven't the correct change, miss, I think I can split you a note.'

'It's all right.' Mary produced a shilling and two sixpences. 'Now, when do you want to see me again, Sid?'

He looked dumbly at Stella Kaye. She managed a brief smile.

'Oh, you won't need any more

treatment. That is the wonderful part of Mr. Pettifer's methods. The complaint is cured by one visit only.'

'Oh, dear!' Mary looked disappointed and tried to appear simple enough to believe that. Pettifer didn't think she was, obviously. He avoided her eyes when she glanced at him in appeal. 'Well, look here,' she went on eagerly, 'my mother suffers dreadfully from what the doctors say is fibrositis, though you'd call it tension, Sid, I know. When can I bring her along to have a treatment?'

Pettifer, lighting another cigarette, coughed nervously through the smoke. 'It's a bit difficult to say.' He hesitated. 'I mean, me present plans . . . No, it's a bit difficult, luv.'

Stella Kaye said incisively, 'Mr. Pettifer is not accepting any more patients at the moment. That is definite.'

'I see.' Mary tucked her bag under one arm. 'Anyway, thanks for what you've done for me, Sid. Be seeing you again sometime, I hope. Cheeriho, Mrs. — er — '

Pettifer made no move to open the

door for her. Mary clicked the Yale lock shut behind her and went, very quietly, down the first flight of stairs. Here she paused, tucking herself into a curve of the banisters, out of sight from the landing above. She was almost instantly rewarded by hearing Pettifer's door open, and, after a brief interval, close again. Somebody — and she only needed one guess — was making sure she was not listening outside that door. Mary's pretty lips formed the word 'Bitch!' as she continued downstairs.

There was a cafe across the street and she felt an urgent need for a drink. She sat down at an empty table in the window embrasure of the cafe and ordered from a waitress who looked as if she would be more at home in a gypsy caravan.

The coffee she ordered was surprisingly good. Mary sipped it thirstily. She hoped she'd got something worthwhile for Chief Inspector Hallam — at some cost to herself, she realized, as she moved incautiously on her chair and felt the tenderness of the muscles on which Pettifer had concentrated. She kept an eye lifted on the street doorway of the block opposite, and, just as she was about to order a second coffee, she saw Pettifer and Mrs. Kaye come out. The woman had her hand on Pettifer's arm, she was smiling at him, though he looked somewhat sullen.

They walked to a Zephyr parked at the kerb, Mrs. Kaye went round to the driver's door, unlocked it and settled in. She leaned across to free the opposite lock and Pettifer got in beside her.

Mary heard a choked-back sob somewhere behind her shoulder. She looked round and saw the waitress standing there, her fists clenched at her sides.

'Something wrong?' Mary asked gently.

The girl spoke in a low, furious tone.

'I'd just like to murder somebody, that's all.'

'Man or woman?' Mary asked idly.

'Both of 'em.' The waitress watched the Zephyr pull smoothly out into the river of traffic.

16

'So you survived the ordeal,' Hallam said. 'Sit down and tell us all about it. In your own words — I don't want Courtroom stuff.'

After the irritating formalities of a morning's desk-work it was pleasant, he found, to lean back and listen to a pretty girl telling a story in a vivacious voice, her phrasing nicely touched with humour.

'Good,' he said when she had finished. 'You've given us a very clear picture. Now we'll probe into the background a bit.

'You see,' he went on, 'I'm interested in this chap because he's quite out of place in Granville Road. Furthermore, I've some reason to think he's a bit of a queer with women. A sexual sadist, if you get that.'

'Oh, yes, sir, we did a course in abnormal psychology at training school. And I think you're right about Pettifer. There was that point, just before Mrs.

Kaye made her dramatic entrance, when he was getting himself terrifically worked up.'

'But, sir!' Spratt protested. 'A chap like that, he wouldn't last five minutes in his so-called healing job!'

'That would depend on the women patients, don't you think, Mary?'

'I do, sir. I would say Pettifer would choose fairly carefully. I mean, he'd have to get a bit of the old come-on from them first. I gave him some of that myself,' she added demurely. 'After all, that's what I was there for, I believe.'

Hallam stirred in his chair. 'I've got to ask you a personal question. I'd like an accurate answer if you feel you can give it. What were your own reactions to this — er — special treatment? Did you find it at all pleasant, exciting?'

'I certainly didn't, sir,' Mary returned promptly. 'When it began to hurt — really hurt — I just felt mad.' She paused thoughtfully for a moment. 'Maybe a little insulted, too, if that's the word I want. I mean, it was as if he was breaking down my dignity as an adult, making me into a smacked child again.'

Hallam leaned forward to scribble on his desk pad.

'Apart from all that, would you say Pettifer was a fairly normal type?'

'Oh, yes, sir. And, though he's far too big-headed about it, I'd say there is something in this gift of healing he claims to have. I don't mean it runs out of his fingers, as he'd like you to think it does, but he knows his massage.'

'Right. Now — Mrs. Kaye. Put the microscope on her for us, will you?'

'I'd judge Mrs. Kaye, sir, to be a very possessive person. Possessive people are always selfish, too. She seems to have taken Pettifer up, and she's going to see to it that no other woman gets anywhere near him. She warned me off all right. And she made me overpay for the treatment. She also made it very clear she didn't want me to see lover-boy again. It was obvious, too, she was aware of Pettifer's little weakness.'

'One more question and then we can all get some lunch,' Hallam said. 'Do you think, if Pettifer were badly thwarted in his — er — abnormal tastes, he would resort to violence to gain his ends?'

'Couldn't say, sir,' Mary replied promptly. 'I only know I'd like to have seen him try it on me.'

'Quite. Well, you've done a good job of work, Mary, and I'll see Superintendent Holmes knows about it.' Mary flushed with pleasure, got up smartly and told Spratt not to bother to see her out.

When Hallam and he had finished their canteen soup and were tackling sausage and mash, with peas, Spratt said, 'Think he might have done it, after all, sir?'

'I don't know, Jack. I just don't know. With a type like Pettifer, where are you? Trying to follow his mind is like getting yourself out of the Australian bush when you're completely lost and haven't a compass. You don't know which way to turn, nor where this or that faint track is likely to lead you. It seems to me, in such baffling territory, only the services of an expert explorer can get you anywhere.'

Spratt hacked furiously at a gristly piece of his sausage.

'Puzzle, find the explorer,' he grunted.

'There's a man in the Department of Psychology at the University. Professor Myers. I'll give him a ring after lunch, before we run out to Granville Road again.'

'Look, sir. Suppose Madge Adkin — the Kayes' house was recorded twice in her diary — interrupted Pettifer in some funny business with Mrs. Kaye? Hold on, though. When we talked with the husband, he just about proved a break-in would be impossible, didn't he?'

'You checked it yourself,' Hallam reminded him. 'And that's another odd factor. If the house numbers were records of Madge's successes, she must have been in Kaye's house twice. However, this afternoon we'll work on those house numbers Madge didn't record. It's possible it was one of those she visited on the night of her death.'

Spratt nodded. 'And so she never had a chance to put it in the diary, of course.'

Three-quarters of an hour later Spratt parked their car in Ashwood Road. He took out his notebook.

'If we work downhill, sir, it's Brown's, Number Two, first. He's a traveller for a china-manufacturing firm. Wife, no family.'

They left the car, turned into Granville Road and went through the gates of a drive on which a big car, very dusty, was standing. Before Spratt's finger had connected with the front-door bellpush, a high, frenzied yapping filled the house within.

A woman's voice chided, 'Quiet, Liselle! Come here!' The noise ceased but racketed out again when the door was opened by a vividly-beautiful young woman with rich auburn hair and entrancing emerald eyes. She held a struggling black poodle in her arms.

Hallam told her who they were, raising his voice above the poodle's din which the woman tried to soften by shaking the animal violently. The policemen understood by her gestures that they were to come in.

As soon as the door closed behind them, the frantic yapping stopped, the woman put the dog down and it proceeded to fawn upon the visitors as if, all its life, it had been awaiting their coming.

'She always does that,' her mistress explained. 'Raises Cain whenever there's a knock, but as soon as I ask anybody in, she knows they are friends and wants to welcome them.'

'Intelligent creatures, poodles,' Hallam said. 'You are Mrs. Brown?' At her nod he continued, 'Is your husband at home?'

'He's mowing the back lawn — I'll fetch him.' She opened a door and motioned them into a bright, newly-furnished lounge. The poodle trotted in with them.

'Not long married, obviously,' Spratt said, gazing around. 'My wife would break the Tenth Commandment if she were here. Good choice, though. Modern but not outrageously contemporary.'

The door opened and a handsome, fair-haired man in his middle twenties came in, smiling. He wore a white shirt, olive slacks and brown canvas shoes. He had the extroverted manner of the successful 'rep.'

'Mr. Brown?' Hallam returned the smile. 'Sorry to be troublesome on a Saturday afternoon, but we shouldn't have to keep you long. I'm in charge of the investigations concerning the death of Miss Madge Adkin.'

'Ah,' Brown answered, 'my wife told me about that.' He pulled chairs forward. 'Most weeks I'm away from home, Monday morning till Friday afternoon, so the local news has to wait until I get back. A very terrible tragedy indeed. I didn't know her at all well, but Molly — my wife — had a nodding acquaintance with her. Molly tells me you people have already been round, making inquiries. She wasn't able to help the man who questioned her.'

'We're pursuing a rather different line now, sir. We have some reason to think a night prowler has been operating in the district. Have you ever suffered here in that respect? No burglaries, no signs of someone having been around — I don't necessarily mean on the night of Miss Adkin's death, my men have already cleared that with your wife, but any time recently?'

'Not while I've been at home,' Brown replied promptly. 'And Molly hasn't complained. As a matter of fact, Chief Inspector, if I were a crook, thinking of burglary around here, this is the last house I'd pick on. There's a brilliant street-lamp on the main road just outside here, and, better still from our point of view, there's this lady.' He rubbed the poodle's ears.

'She's a good watchdog?'

'The best. It's one of the reasons we got her, me being away so much and Molly on her own. The slightest noise on our premises, outside as well as in, will set Liselle off.'

'Fair enough,' Hallam returned. 'We'll move along, and let you get back to the lawn.'

Five doors lower down, at their next call, they found an elderly man on his knees before a flower border. He rose to greet them, a big, well-made fellow with a thatch of silvered hair and a keen, hawk-like face.

'Mr. Stewart?' Hallam asked.

'Aye. Duncan Stewart.' The reply held

a certain suspicious wariness.

Hallam said his piece while Stewart, with his head on one side, listened attentively.

'I wis an electrical engineer before I retired,' Stewart said when the policeman had finished. 'And I've no' saved ma siller all ma life to hae some criminal whup it awa'. If ye'll step into the hoose I'll show ye whit I mean.'

Twenty minutes later Hallam and Spratt made their farewells to the Scotsman, both a trifle dizzy with his technical talk of contact breakers, magnetic fields and electronic rays. They were also fully convinced that of all the private houses, shops and warehouses in Deniston, Number Twelve Granville Road was the hardest for even an expert burglar to tackle. There were alarms, carefully set each night by Stewart, on all the doors and windows, in addition to the locks and bolts with which each of these possible means of entry was fitted. Hallam had been invited to walk from the kitchen to the front door along a central passage after Stewart had flipped a switch. He had only taken a few steps when a bell began to scream like a demented siren. What was more, skilfully-put questions had elicited the fact that Madge Adkin had known all about Stewart's precautions. He was so proud of them that Hallam guessed most of his neighbours shared the same information.

'You can write him off,' Hallam told Spratt. 'Who's next?'

'Next door down. George Gower, dental mechanic. Wife and one son of school age.'

There was no reply to their ring, but when they went round the side of the house they found the Gowers at the far end of a weedy, neglected garden. The boy was lazily propelling himself back and forth on a swing suspended from a tree branch, his parents were seated in deck chairs, each with a book. A fat, sleepy black and white mongrel dog lay at the woman's side.

Gower looked up, saw them approaching and said something to his wife as he got to his feet. When he discovered what they wanted he led them back to the house. Of all the dwellings they had visited, this was the most uncared-for. The outside paintwork was peeling and a dislodged roof-tile partly blocked a gutter. There was a long transverse crack in one of the side windows, and the tongue of the Yale lock in the front door was so worn that Spratt was able to spring the catch from outside with a firm push of his shoulder.

'Oh, I know,' Gower said with a shrug of excuse when they pointed the deficiencies out to him. He was a small, brown-haired man with intelligent eyes and a high, balding forehead. 'But to be perfectly honest, I'm the worst do-it-yourselfer ever. And, somehow, we never seem to get around to having a man in to straighten things up. Both the wife and I are more interested in intellectual things — literature, music, art. Makes a nice change for me after living among sets of dentures all day,' he added with a grin. 'Anyway, we don't possess anything worth pinching.'

'You have a dog,' Hallam said. 'Is he a good house-dog at nights?'

'Him?' Gower laughed heartily. 'He wouldn't wake up if a couple of armies started a battle over his head. He's like the rest of us here — a thinker, not a creature of action.'

'I can't see that chap going for Madge Adkin,' Spratt said as they left Gower's house, 'even if he did find her on his premises. He'd probably have invited her to sit down and listen to a basinful of chamber music. Or have asked her if she'd read any good books lately. West here,' he added as he opened a gate. 'The photographer. Lives with his sister.'

West answered their knock. He grinned expansively when he saw Spratt.

'Come in, Sergeant. And this time you'll damn well have to have that cup of tea you refused yesterday. My sister is just brewing up.' He shook hands with Hallam. 'Glad to know you, Chief Inspector.' He raised his voice. 'Flo! Two more spoonfuls in the pot! We have visitors. That'll fluster her a bit,' he added to the policemen. 'But you mustn't mind her fussiness. My marriage went wrong, you see, and she never landed a man herself. So she came here to keep house for me.'

He led them along the hall into a large, airy lounge with big French windows. Apart from a slight leaning towards artiness, the room was tastefully decorated. As they entered, a handsome smooth-coated black retriever rose from the hearthrug and greeted them politely.

Hallam complimented West on the dog's condition as the photographer found them chairs.

'Yes, he's pretty fit, is Jerry,' West replied. 'Right, boy, you can lie down now. A dog like that needs bags of exercise and I see he gets it. Walk miles with him.' He sprang up to open the door and to introduce his sister, as the plain, angular woman whom Spratt had already met pushed a laden tea-trolley into the room.

'No, please don't go,' Hallam said when Miss West, having seen them all served, murmured something about leaving them to talk business. 'Our errand concerns you both. You've already had a visit earlier this week from one of my men, making inquiries into Miss Adkin's death?'

'Yes,' West said, 'but we weren't able to give him any relevant information.'

'We're wondering about strangers being around that night. What's the dog like as a watch-keeper?'

'Excellent. We could go to sleep here at nights with every door and window left open, and I'd stake my oath Jerry would alarm us at the least sound he couldn't account for. He's not normally a noisy dog in daytime — retrievers aren't — but he'd raise hell at night.'

'Only if strangers were about, though, I suppose?'

'He'd do it with anybody. Not out of stupidity, you know, but just because he'd realize, if someone he knew did come around after normal hours, that it would be in an emergency, and we'd want to know about it.'

Miss West spoke with a nervous rush of words.

'There was that time early in the spring when Mrs. Benton, one of our neighbours, was taken ill with acute appendicitis. Mr. Benton woke Christine — that's the daughter — and sent her round here to use our phone, as they haven't one of their own. Jerry barked his head off even before Christine reached the front door. And they're ever such good friends, really.'

'Yes, the old boy absolutely adores that kid,' West agreed. 'And yet — well, you see. Somebody he knew well, who's always popping in here at odd times during the day. But something was up — he sensed it — and there you are. And you needn't get all big-headed about it, either,' he told the dog, which had risen upon hearing its name and stood looking from one to the other of them in mild inquiry, its feathery tail moving gently. 'You lie down and don't listen to what you're not supposed to hear.'

Some few minutes later, when his sister had gone back to the kitchen for more hot water, West leant forward.

'About that act of mine on the Common. Look here, I realize it was a silly thing to do. Damned childish, as a matter of fact.'

'We're not pursuing the matter officially,' Hallam said. 'But if you feel like making amends, I'd suggest you apologize to the parties concerned, and let it stay at that.'

'Apologize to Newton?' West laughed. 'He'd think I was mad. He doesn't understand apologies. And as for Stella Kaye, I wouldn't be seen dead near her.' He bent to pat the retriever. 'It's dogs I'm fond of, not bloody bitches!'

17

Benton answered their ring at Number Twenty-two. His thick-lensed spectacles flashed as he looked up at them, chin out aggressively.

'Come in,' he said loudly. 'I want a few words with you.'

He almost pushed them into the dining-room. 'Sit down if you wish,' he said and drew out two leather-seated, straight-backed chairs from the table, and perched himself on the high window-seat, his back to the light.

'Have you come to tell me you have tracked down the man who sexually assaulted my daughter?'

'Why, no, sir,' Hallam said soothingly. 'This is another matter. It may be connected with the complaint you made, but, at the moment — '

'You needn't go on,' Benton grated. 'You've done nothing, that's obvious. And excuses are no use to me.'

'Now, sir,' Hallam protested mildly, 'please be reasonable. We didn't ignore your complaint, by any means. We have made close inquiries in the district and we have had a man watching the Common. In my experience of such cases the offender rarely, if ever, operates a second time in the same area, without an interval. He lies low, you know, until the heat is off.'

Benton's dumpy body shifted impatiently.

'Talk like that is cheap, Chief Inspector. But it gets you nowhere. You won't catch this fellow by negative methods. I'd very much like to lay hands on him myself, but as that isn't likely, I can at least, by scaring him off, stop him from attacking innocent young girls again.'

'Just how do you propose to do that, *sir?*'

'By getting in touch with the local press, inviting a reporter and a photographer up here and letting Christine make a detailed statement to them. I shall then put forward a scheme, which I am prepared to organize personally, for a posse of local residents to patrol the Common and stop this menace. I shall make it clear that we are forced to take this action since police surveillance is woefully inadequate. I intend to do this at once today, in fact.'

'If I may make a suggestion, sir,' Spratt put in as the little man paused for breath, 'I'd leave it till tomorrow. That way, you'll be sure of getting plenty of space in the paper. There's never much doing over the weekend, and the paper is hard to fill on a Monday.'

'You're right, Sergeant,' Hallam weighed in. 'And when you ring up, *sir*, ask to be put through to Denis Overton. He's the crime reporter and he'll do you very well.'

Benton put his head on one side, frowning at them. 'You mean you want me to take this action?'

'Actually, no,' Hallam replied, 'but we've no power to stop you, you see. If you want publicity in this, you'll just have to go ahead.' He glanced at his wrist-watch. 'Shall we leave the subject, and deal with the real reason for our call here this afternoon? You have a dog, I believe, sir?'

'I have. A Scots terrier named Fiona. Getting on a bit in years, but quite an excellent companion. But her licence is paid and she never goes out collarless.'

'Would you say she's a good watch-dog, sir? Especially at nights?'

'I would.'

'And how are you for security here? You see everything is locked up when you go to bed, windows fastened and so on?'

'I do. But what on earth is all this about?'

'Just checking, sir. And now we'll get on our way.'

Hallam paused in the act of pushing his chair back. He had caught the faint sound of a footfall in the passage outside. But there were no signs of another human presence as, in studied silence, Benton saw them out.

'Nice chap, that,' Spratt commented as they went through the drive gate. 'Wonderful companion for a day at the seaside, I should think. Rennisons now, sir?'

But the old couple were out. Though Hallam and Spratt walked round the side of the semi-detached house they could see no easy way of ingress. 'Just possible, but unlikely,' Hallam decided.

They went back to their car in Ashwood Road. Spratt waited until a taxi, coming from the direction of the city, swung in front of them into Granville Road. Putting the car into motion then, he said, 'We don't seem to have much luck.'

'No,' Hallam agreed, feeling for his pipe. 'Look, Jack. We'll go back to the office and run over the facts together. It won't take long. Sunday tomorrow gives those facts, such as they are, a chance to sort themselves out in the old subconscious. We'll make a fresh start on Monday.'

'Did you fix that appointment with Professor Myers, sir ?'

'Yes. Eleven-thirty at his office on Monday. Let's hope something'll come of it.'

Hallam found several new items on his desk when they reached Headquarters, he flicked through them and decided they could all wait over the weekend.

'Right,' he said when he and Spratt had settled themselves. 'Why was she killed? Four possibilities — homicidal maniac wandering around, Fred Mitchell silencing her because she recognized him as a con on the run, a love-affair which ended stickily, an irate householder dealing too severely, by accident or design, with a midnight intruder. Your throw, Jack.'

'No evidence for the maniac, though we do have this queer on the common. Mitchell might have, but why should he have been wandering about at that time of night? Indications of love-affair, nil. Which leaves us with the householder.'

'You have your list there?'

'I'll take them from the top, those she hadn't recorded, and assume it was a man who did Madge — women don't usually strangle. Brown was away from home and the poodle would have given the alarm, anyway. She just couldn't have broken into Stewart's place. Gower — possible, but that easy-going type, well, would he? As I said before. West — I'm not sure, considering his antics on the Common. But could Madge have charmed his dog into silence? Benton — no, again. Rennison? Too old. Hasn't the strength to finish off a big woman like Madge. So, if we're not going to consider she met trouble when she was operating on the opposite side of Granville Road, the odd-numbers side, that brings us to the Kayes.'

'I can't see anybody, on that opposite side, killing her and carting the body round to a garden facing Gypsy Lane, Jack.'

'No more can I, sir, unless it was from one of the houses near the bottom.' He consulted his sketch-plan. 'Levitt, the pork butcher, could have done that. Or the chap next door, Dalby. Or even Sowden, next to him.'

'I suppose we'd better do a recheck on that side. Going back to the others, though. You've visited every house there now. With due allowances for individual differences, there's one common factor in all of them, bar two.'

Spratt nodded. 'You mean, sir, they seem to be normal suburban families, more or less? They fit into the recognized pattern. With the exception of West and the Kaye family.'

'Yes. Of course, there are the Cranes. We mustn't forget them because they don't actually live in Granville Road. Nor the Tanners. Crane comes from a better background than most of the Ashwood-ites, just as Tanner comes from a less-cultured one. But they still fit, to me. You'll always find a jobbing gardener in a suburban community, and generally somebody is taking advantage of the 'my girl rides' status symbol. They're just as much a part as the milkman and postman.

'West, now. Odd, but perhaps only because he has an unusual job, is at home when most men are out at work. And what's Hecuba to him, or he to Hecuba? Hamlet, Jack.'

'We did it at school, sir. I get the idea.'

'But the Kayes. What about them?'

'Odd only because of Pettifer, I'd say. Different from the others because — well, sir, it's as if they'd gone in for an unusual pet. While the others keep a dog or a cat, or maybe a couple of rabbits or a tortoise for the kids, they've got a ruddy great cheetah.'

Hallam grinned. 'I could make a pun on that.' His face grew ruefully solemn. 'Fact is, the Kayes are the only point we have to hammer at, as far as I can see. Actually, that means Pettifer.'

'Mrs. Kaye alibied him. Collusion there, do you think?'

'I'd suspect it, if only I could see some reason why Pettifer should want to put Madge out. Surely she hadn't anything on him we don't know about? But why did Madge note down Kaye's number twice, when we know she couldn't have done a break-in there? I'm sure we'd find a scent if we knew those answers.'

'I've been thinking about that last one, sir. Could it have been possible that Madge, hearing the Pellings' views of the so-called scandalous goings-on there, was merely doing a bit of spying and listening from outside, to satisfy the curiosity the Pellings had roused in her?'

'Now, that's quite an idea, Jack. But the hell with it! Let's pack it in for now. We're sitting here gazing at a crossword puzzle where none of the clues make sense. They may look clearer on Monday morning.'

'Or one of them may, sir. It often happens, when you're doing a crossword, you see one answer and put it in and then you find you can build the rest of the puzzle on that one.'

'Roll on the master clue, then,' Hallam said fervently.

18

Spratt had already gone and Hallam was about to leave his office when the desk sergeant appeared.

'There's a chap outside, sir. A taxi-driver, name of Bryant. He's asking to see you personally. It's in connection with the Adkin case. Says a Mr. Kaye told him he must see you.'

'Show him in, Sergeant.' Hallam went back to his desk.

The man who was ushered in was short and fat but he moved lightly, quickly. He took the chair Hallam indicated, placed his peaked hat on the floor at his feet and spoke without waste of words.

'Martin Bryant, sir. Employed by the Get-U-There Taxi Company. I work from the Dean Street rank. This afternoon a young woman I know, name of Dora North, asked me to take a friend of hers out to Granville Road, where he was living. The man was Sidney Pettifer. He runs a sort of massage place in Dean Street. He was drunk.'

He paused until Hallam's pencil ceased to move across his desk pad.

'I didn't fancy the job, sir, but Dora's a pal of mine and she was worried about him. We got him downstairs and into the back of the cab. He had a bottle of whisky, about two-thirds empty, in his hand. I tried to get it away from him but he wouldn't be parted from it.

'Well, sir, I promised Dora I'd see him all right and we set off. He was at the maudlin stage, wouldn't stop talking. He kept saying, over and over, 'I didn't mean to hurt her. She wasn't nothing to me. I didn't mean to squeeze her neck like that.' Then he'd lean forward and grab my shoulder and say, 'You gotta believe me, pal. I didn't mean it — I swear I didn't.'

'I was glad when we got to this address in Granville Road. A gentleman came out of the house and I helped him to get Pettifer upstairs and on to a bed, where he went out like a light. But all the way up he was going on as he had done in the cab, and when he paid me off, this Mr. Kaye — he told me his name — asked me how long Pettifer had been like that so I told him and he said, 'It's important you should let Detective Chief Inspector Hallam of the C.I.D. know about this at once. You must go and see him.' And then I remembered that Ashwood strangling case.

'I checked with my office manager when I got back to Dean Street, and he agreed I ought to see you, sir. I don't know if you think it's important or not?'

'I'm very pleased indeed you came, Mr. Bryant,' Hallam said warmly. 'Though I must ask you not to talk to anyone about this.'

'You can depend on it I won't, sir.'

'You say Pettifer was clean out when you left him?'

'That's a fact, sir. He won't be conscious this side of tomorrow morning.'

'Right.' Hallam thanked him again, saw him out. Then he came back to his desk and studied the notes he had made.

Five minutes later he got up and

reached for his hat. There was nothing else he could do that night.

But at nine o'clock the following morning he was back at his office, and so was Jack Spratt, digesting the story his chief inspector had to tell.

'So I decided to send for him this morning, Jack, and a patrol car has gone there now.' Hallam looked quizzically at his sergeant. 'You're probably cussing me like fury, dragging you down here on one of your off-duty Sundays.'

Spratt shrugged. 'All part of the life, sir.'

'I'll see it's made up to you. Well, back to last night. You'll notice one point. Kaye seemed very keen to land Pettifer in the stew.'

'Maybe him coming home drunk upset Kaye. Let him see what the chap really was like.'

But a knock at the door and the entrance of a constable saved Hallam from commenting.

'Sidney Pettifer outside, sir.'

'Good. Fire him in, Dawes.'

The healer had a purple bruise on his

forehead and he had not shaved. His eyes were bleared and he moved his lips and tongue ceaselessly against the foul taste in his mouth. He collapsed limply into the chair to which Dawes guided him, sank his head in his hands and groaned.

'What the hell's the idea, dragging me down here at this hour of a Sunday morning?' he moaned.

'Not feeling too good, Mr. Pettifer?' Hallam asked. 'How about some strong coffee before we talk?'

'You can stuff yer bloody coffee.'

'Thank you.' Hallam's voice hardened. 'You know why you are here?'

'Like 'ell I do. Nobody's told me nothing.' Pettifer raised his head carefully and glared at Hallam.

'Yesterday afternoon, Mr. Pettifer — '

'Yeah, I know. I got proper stinking. But that's no bloody crime, is it?'

'You were shooting your mouth all the way home in the taxi. You kept saying you'd strangled somebody — a woman.'

Pettifer's eyes opened widely. 'I was saying — what?'

'You heard me. And you'd better

explain yourself.'

Pettifer rubbed a hand over his face. 'Look, I don't know nothing about this. I can't remember . . . They put me into the taxi and then . . . No, it's no good. I don't remember nothing after that.

'See, I'll tell you what happened. Yest'day after dinner — lunch, I mean — the phone rang. Reg and the kids was in the garden, Stella was upstairs. So I answers the ring and it were for me, as it happened. Friend of mine wanted to see me urgent. Said she had something nice for me. So I ses right, I'd see her at Dean Street in half an hour. And I nips out and catches the bus.'

'You didn't tell either of the Kayes where you were going?'

Pettifer licked his dry lips with a discoloured tongue.

'No. Well, you see, Stella — she's a bit possessive, like, and I'd promised I wouldn't see this girl no more.'

'Right. Please go on.'

'Well, I meet Dora and we have ourselves a talk. If yer don't believe me, ask her. She lives at Four Yeoman Row.

We got a few things straightened out. She'd brought me a bottle of Scotch.' He stopped, listening, like Hallam and Spratt, to a commotion in the outer office. The duty sergeant's voice seemed to be reasoning with a flood of shrill female protestations. A constable knocked at the door and put his head in.

'A Mrs. Kaye is here, sir. She insists on seeing you at once.'

'Would you ask her to come in?'

Stella Kaye, it appeared, had left home in a tearing hurry. Her blonde hair was in some disarray, her lipstick merely smudged on her mouth. She went straight to Pettifer, who had backed against a wall, and put her hands on his shoulders.

'What have they been doing to you, Sid? Why have they brought you here? When I woke up this morning and Reg told me the police had taken you away, I just had to come down here, Sid, to look after you.'

'They're trying to frame me for something or other. It don't make any sense to me. But you'll back me up, won't you, pet?'

Hallam broke in, addressing the grinning Dawes.

'Show Mr. Pettifer into the interview room, please. I may need a signed statement from him after I have talked to Mrs. Kaye.'

The woman swung round on him.

'I'm staying with Sid, wherever he goes.'

'If you wish to help him,' Hallam told her crisply, 'You'll best do so if my instructions are carried out.'

'Oh, all right!' The assent was ungracious, a scowl and a petulant shrug accompanied it. Pettifer was ushered out and Hallam nodded at the vacant chair.

'Sit down, Mrs. Kaye. This shouldn't take long.' He waited until she had settled herself. 'You know, I suppose, why we asked Mr. Pettifer to come here this morning?'

'My husband said something about him confessing to the Adkin woman's murder. That's absurd, of course. You've no right to accuse him of such a thing.'

'He has been accused of nothing, Mrs. Kaye. Let's be factual. We merely wished to clear up one or two conflicting pieces of evidence. You can help by answering a few questions.' Again came the sulky shrug. 'You were at home when your guest returned yesterday?'

'Yes. Oh, I know he was in a sorry state but you've got to realize that a man like him, with his wonderfully super-normal gift of healing, can't be judged by ordinary standards.'

'So you were not shocked, nor disgusted, because he had come back helplessly drunk?'

'It's none of your business what I felt about it. You're as bad as my husband. Last night he said we should tell Sid to leave the house and go back to his own place, because what he called 'this sort of thing' wasn't good for the boys to know about. Well, we had a row, if you must know, and it brought on one of my collapses and I had to go to bed with sleeping tablets. Sid Pettifer had nothing to do with this Adkin business and if you can't see that you must be the dimmest ever.'

'What we are trying to do, Mrs. Kaye,

is to eliminate Mr. Pettifer, as a suspect, if we can. We have his story, and we hope to check it with the lady who was in his company yesterday.'

He might have struck her across the face with all the force of his arm. Her head jerked back.

'Lady?' She snapped the word like a rat-trap springing shut. 'What lady?'

'I am not at liberty to mention names. If you wish to know, you must ask Mr. Pettifer.'

'I'll do that all right. So he was with a woman! And I thought he'd just had the urge to go on a bender!' She jumped to her feet. 'I want to see him — now!'

'You can take him home with you if you wish.' Hallam had had enough of her. 'If I need a statement from him, I'll get one later, when he is in a better condition to give it.'

'Was it that Dora North Sid was with?'

Hallam didn't bother to reply. He rang for Dawes, and when he and Spratt were alone again the sergeant looked up from the notes he had been taking.

'Well, sir, anything in it?'

Hallam shrugged. 'I'm open to bet the 'confession' the taxi-driver and Kaye heard didn't refer to Madge Adkin at all.'

'Ah!' Spratt snapped his fingers. 'Pettifer was meaning that go he had at Dora, which Ted Walsh told us about. The drink had made him maudlin, softened him up on Dora, who'd been nice enough to buy him whisky.'

'That's how I see it. But we'd better contact Dora as soon as possible. Will you do that?'

'I'll go now, sir. She ought to be up, time I get there.'

Alone, Hallam sat staring before him until Dawes came in again.

'We have a Mr. West outside, sir. He wants to see you.'

'Chap from Granville Road?'

'Yes, sir.'

'I'll see him now.'

West was less sure of himself this morning. He seemed taut, worried, as he sat down.

'It's about Christine Benton, Chief Inspector. She said she was assaulted by a man on the Common. Now, look, you've got to make allowances for the kid. She didn't mean any harm. The fact is, her story was a make-up from start to finish. There wasn't any man. There wasn't any assault.'

Hallam smiled. 'I was moving towards the same conclusion myself, Mr. West.'

'Well, it was like this. Her father, who can be a bit of a swine when he likes, insisted she took riding lessons at Crane's place. She wasn't at all keen and in the end Crane threw her out, and knowing her, I'd say Christine was probably to blame there. She's at a difficult age.

'So she had to go home and tell pop, and he was furious with her. Gave her merry hell, it seems. And he does go on and on. I mean, he won't say his piece and leave it alone.

'The kid went on to the Common, pretty upset. And she got the fool idea of coming home with this story about a lecherous bloke there. Thought it would divert the old man's wrath over the riding business. Give him something else to think about. That part worked.

'He dragged her down here to see you.

She was stuck with her story now and had to sweat it out. And then Benton got the idea of bringing the Press in. That scared Christine properly. So she came to me yesterday evening and spilt the beans, asked me what she should do. I said she must tell her father. She promised she would. Then I went along to the Bentons to persuade him not to blame her too much. In fact, I told him a few home truths. He crumpled fairish and admitted he didn't like the idea of having to let you people know the facts. He said it would make him look such a fool. So I promised to tell you, first thing this morning.'

'Why did Christine come to you before she told her parents?'

'Well, you see, we've known her practically all her life. She's always made our house her second home. Marriage passed my sister by, so I suppose the kiddie filled some need, and I've always been 'Uncle Colin' to her.'

'Which was probably why, Mr. West, when we asked to describe this man, she gave us a picture which fitted you in several details. You'd be the first man she'd think of.'

'Ah!' West waggled a finger. 'And a psychiatrist would talk about subconscious desires, wouldn't he? These kids grow up faster than you realize.'

Hallam said, 'Thanks for coming. It's cleared up one of my little worries.'

'And will anything be — er — made of it?'

'Not by us. It's a matter we shall wipe off the slate completely.' He got up to see his visitor out. 'I only wish I could sponge out a few more as easily, Mr. West!'

19

Yeoman Row was a dingy street of back-to-back houses between the docks and the outer business perimeter on the eastern side of the city. The houses of Yeoman Row were small and crowded, but most of their inhabitants had pride in their dwellings. They made the best of what there was.

Spratt left his car on the main road, and, walking into Yeoman Row, saw every indication that it was still sunk in late Sunday-morning slumber.

However, his knock at Number Four brought an immediate response in the person of a handsome, dark-haired man in his early thirties. He was freshly shaved and wore a dark blue shirt and grey flannels. His eyes widened as he stared at his visitor.

'Sergeant Spratt! What you doing here? Look, I'm going level now. I told you so, when you got on to me over that Rutland

Street break-in. You've no cause to come here at this time of a Sunday morning!'

Spratt grinned. 'Take it easy, Dan. I'm not seeking you. I want a word with your sister Dora.'

'She hasn't done anything. She's a good girl, is Dora. Always has been.'

'Sure, Dan. But I'm checking on a fellow she was with yesterday afternoon. Won't take a minute.'

'Better come in, then.' Dan North stood aside and Spratt stepped straight from the street into the single living-room. It was small, and crowded with a table, half a dozen chairs, a television set and a large treadle-worked sewing machine. But the worn carpet was clean, and the table, which bore the remains of breakfast, was covered with a snow-white cloth.

'Dora's still abed,' Dan said. 'Having a lie-in. So's me wife, Coral. Me, I never was one to stay in bed in the mornings.' He moved towards a door in the corner of the room. 'I'd better get Dora up, then.'

The door opened on to a carpeted

staircase, Dan went up and returned after a brief interval.

'She says she won't be long, Sarge.'

He sat down opposite Spratt.

'This chap you mentioned, would it be Sid Pettifer, by any chance?'

'It is, Dan. You know him?'

'I've met him. Dora brought him home here a few times. Not lately, though. 'Fact, me and Coral thought she'd gone off him. Seems we were a bit too optimistic.'

'That sounds as if you don't like him much.'

'We don't. There's something odd about that character. Is he in trouble?'

'Not exactly. He's mixed up with something a bit funny, that's all.'

'Women!' Dan said. 'You can't tell 'em, can you?' He cocked an ear. 'Here she comes.'

Dora wore a long scarlet dressing gown over flowered pyjamas. She had run a comb through her thick wavy black hair and though she had no make-up on, she looked fresh enough without it.

Spratt said good morning. Dora nodded

and took the chair her brother hooked out from under the table with one foot. Spratt sat down again.

'Miss North,' he said. 'I understand you spent some of yesterday afternoon with Mr. Sidney Pettifer.'

'That's right,' Dora answered pertly. 'Is there a law against it?'

'Any day now, likely,' Spratt responded. 'Look, here's the point. Was Pettifer really and truly tight when you put him in that taxi?'

'Yes, and it was all my fault, giving him the stuff. See, I was out to do him a dirty trick, send him home drunk and get him into trouble with that Granville Road lot. This morning, that doesn't seem very clever.'

'Did you talk to him about that strangling case at Ashwood?'

She shook her head. 'Never mentioned it. Nor did he.'

'He said nothing about it, either sober or drunk?'

'Not a word.' Dora was looking puzzled, but Spratt did not enlighten her.

'Thanks,' he said, and got to his feet.

'Well, that's all, I think, Miss North. Sorry to have dragged you out of bed. But I had to check what Pettifer told us, and you've been most helpful.'

'But wait a minute. Something I want to show you.' Her hand went to the pocket of her dressing gown. She pulled out two envelopes and threw them on the table. 'Look at that lot,' she said to Spratt.

The sergeant sat down again. He picked up one of the envelopes and saw the typewritten address was to Miss Dora North, c/o The Comfy Cafe, Dean Street. The postmark was dated ten days earlier. Carefully, he took out the single sheet the envelope contained. Its message was also typewritten, with neither heading address nor salutation.

'If you want your boyfriend back act quick. Him and his latest woman is lovers.'

The second letter was identically addressed, its postmark dated the previous Friday. Its typed sheet also bore two sentences: 'You been told. Act quick before its to late.'

Spratt looked up to find both Dora and

her brother watching him intently.

'Any idea where these came from?'

The girl shook her head. 'I don't know anybody who has a typewriter or who could get to one. Of course, we've got one in the office at the caff, but those weren't done on it. I checked. Got Gladys to type me a few lines and compared 'em. There were lots of little differences — you know. Besides, look how our place is spelt on the envelopes. That's wrong. I mean, it's right, really, but we don't spell it that way. It's K-u-m-f-i K-a-f-e. The boss says it makes people look twice and it's a bit of a joke, like. I showed them to Sid yesterday and he didn't know anything about them.'

'Do you mind if I borrow them?'

'Take them and welcome, Sergeant. I don't want the things, now I've told Sid about them. Of course, he said it was all lies.'

Spratt put the letters in his pocket. For the second time he stood up to go. But a sharp, insistent knocking on the door stayed him. Dan went to answer it.

'Oh, good morning. We want to see Miss Dora North.' There was an icy aggression in the demand.

'Oh, my God!' Dora clutched at Spratt's sleeve. 'It's that woman! She's come to make a row. What'll I do?'

Spratt patted her hand reassuringly. 'Don't worry, love. You and Dan can handle her between you.'

'But you'll stay, won't you?'

'Aye,' Spratt said dryly, 'maybe I will, then.'

'You'd best come in,' Dan was saying. 'You, too, if you must, chum.'

As Stella Kaye and Pettifer came into the room, Spratt was interested to note that the former had found an opportunity, since he had seen her last, of putting on the complete range of her war-paint. He also marked the contemptuous curl of her lips as she glanced around the small overcrowded room. The glance reached him and at once her mouth tightened.

'What are you doing here?'

'Oh, I get around, madam,' Spratt said with a beaming smile.

'I suppose you've been checking on what Sidney told you about yesterday?

You couldn't take his word for it, of course!'

Spratt's smile became even more expansive.

'No, madam, I couldn't.'

'And have you completed your checking?'

'Yes, madam, I have.'

'In that case there's no need for you to hang around any longer. I wish to speak to Dora North privately.'

Dan came forward from the door.

'Mr. Spratt is a guest here, and this is my house, missus. If he goes, it's either because he wants to, or because I ask him to. And I'm not asking — see?'

Stella Kaye looked at him carefully, for the first time. It was clear she liked what she saw. Her eyes made this especially plain to big, handsome Dan North. She took a step towards him and laid a hand on his arm.

'You're Dora's brother Dan, aren't you? I've heard about you. I'm Stella. Look, I'm sorry to be a nuisance, Dan, but I would like to speak to Dora alone. Okay?' She gave his arm a little squeeze, her fingers spreading on it, pressing it warmly.

Dan shook her off. 'There's only two rooms downstairs in this house, missus,' he said stolidly. 'This and the kitchen. As my wife, like most women, reckons the kitchen's her territory, you'll have to talk here.'

She shrugged petulantly. 'Oh, very well.' She turned to Dora. 'I understand you have been receiving anonymous letters. They make certain statements involving me. I wish to see them.'

Dora hesitated, waiting for Spratt. But the sergeant remained silent. 'I haven't got them any more,' Dora said. 'I got rid of them.'

'You mean you've destroyed them?'

Dora shrugged. 'I didn't see any sense in keeping them.'

'I think you're lying to me.'

'Now, look here, missus,' Dan said angrily. 'Nobody's going to come here and call my sister a liar. Anyway, why're you so bothered about the letters? Because what they said was true, eh?'

'Why, you dirty-minded, low-down

ignorant gypsy!' Temper made her face an ugly mask of fury. 'I'll — '

'Now, now!' Spratt said. 'Let's keep calm. The letters you spoke of have been handed over to me, Mrs. Kaye. As far as you're concerned, that's that. I think it would be a good idea if you and your friend left now.'

'I'll take advice from you when I ask for it! And that won't be for a while!' She swung to Dora again. 'I've one more thing to tell you, miss. Stay away from Sid in future — do you hear? I know what you want — you're out to keep him down, to drag him back to your own level, where he was before he met me. Well, I'll see you don't do that in a million years! Is that clear enough?'

Dora took the fury of the words unflinchingly, but Dan's fists were working at his sides as he took a step towards Pettifer.

'You want to say your little piece, too, mate?' he asked softly. 'You've been standing there long enough, dumb as Coggan's donkey. Or maybe you'd like to walk outside with me?'

Pettifer spluttered inarticulately and shrank towards Stella Kaye. Dan gave a contemptuous snort, crossed to the door and threw it open.

'On your way, the pair of you — and move!' he grated.

'And they went like a couple of lambs,' Spratt told Hallam at the end of the brief report he telephoned from a public box. 'Want me to bring these letters in, sir?'

'Tomorrow morning,' Hallam replied. 'You get off home now, Jack. I've just rung my wife to tell her to hurry up the joint, and neither battle, murder nor sudden death'll keep me from carving it today!'

20

Half a Sabbath's rest brought Hallam to his office on Monday morning refreshed and keen. He dealt swiftly and concisely with the routine matters awaiting him and when Spratt came in Hallam threw down his pen and said, 'Right. Let's be at it.'

'First, here are the letters, sir.'

'Inexpert typist,' Hallam commented. 'And the mis-spellings are interesting. They look phony to me. Done on purpose to suggest an illiteracy which probably wasn't there at all.'

He glanced at his watch.

'Shove these away for now. We're due at the University in a quarter of an hour. I promised Professor Myers we'd be punctual.'

In the entrance hall of Deniston's modern, expanding university, a uniformed porter directed them to the Department of Psychology. They found a bright, expensively-furnished office which still smelt of fresh paint and new carpeting. Two pretty young women worked busily behind electric typewriters. One of them said, 'Yes, of course,' when Hallam stated his business, and she preceded them to a door marked 'Professor David Myers' in white letters.

Myers rose to greet them with outstretched hand and a warmly-welcoming smile. They settled themselves in comfortable armchairs.

'And now, gentlemen,' Myers asked. 'How can I help you?'

'We're dealing with a case of homicide, sir,' Hallam began, 'which has turned up an odd character, a man who may, or may not, be connected with the crime. Both Sergeant Spratt and I have met his type before, but only superficially. We want to know how his mind works, what sort of things he's likely to do. You'll have a precise and technical name for it, but he appears to be the sort of character who gets considerable satisfaction — sexual satisfaction probably — from beating women. Physically, I mean.'

'Ah,' Myers said, 'a sexual sadist. Yes.

They are not uncommon, but they are very unpredictable. I'll do my best if you will give me all the details you can, though, of course, to make a reliable diagnosis I should have to see him.'

'And that's not possible at this stage, sir.'

'I understand.' He pulled a pad towards him and picked up a gold-cased propelling pencil. 'Well, let's see what we can do from long range.'

As briefly as he could, Hallam described Pettifer and his healing claims. He told of the situation at the Kayes', of the cane he had seen there, of Mary Jones's experiences during Pettifer's treatment of her.

'What we are hoping from you, sir,' he concluded, 'is an opinion whether this man could have killed by strangulation, possibly in a fit of rage or even — er — ecstasy, a middle-aged woman who was, we think, a stranger to him.'

Myers said, 'I see,' and studied the notes he had been making. Then he looked up at his visitors.

'You ask for an opinion, and I'll try to give you one.' His voice had taken on a lecture-room resonance. 'Now, we have this man, X, living with family Y in unconventional circumstances. Mrs. Y is apparently dominated by him. The obvious, but not necessarily the true inference is that she is having a sordid affair with him. No doubt you gentlemen, like her neighbours, would argue that, if she decided to run off the rails, why pick X? His manners, his background, his lack of culture, his sub-intellectual pursuits are surely opposite to her own social upbringing. If she merely wanted the normal sexual satisfactions from such a man, there are opportunities in plenty, without bringing him into her home and flaunting him before her husband and children.

'There must therefore be something deeper here than the ordinary affair, a bond between them which overrides normality. We can begin to understand this if we look at the psychological aspects of sexual sadism itself.

'There are several forms of it but we need only consider the type in which we find sadism — cruel acts — related to full sexual pleasure, and here the aggressive emotion replaces what in the normal man would be that of affection. This kind of sexual pleasure is compulsive and although it can be satisfied for a time, the urge invariably recurs.

'Such men seldom marry and when they are subjected to psychoanalysis they show a deeply-rooted subconscious hatred of women, due, in the main, to unkindness, neglect or actual cruelty experienced by them from their mother at an early age. So builds up a fervid, but still repressed and subconscious, desire to get their own back — in the same way — on this monstrous regiment of women.

'If, in later life, such a man can procure some means of having women come to him and put their bodies, as it were, at his mercy, and if he then can wreak vengeance upon them — and our friend X has an ideal set-up for such a purpose — his repressed desire enjoys repeated satisfaction.

'Let us face it, such sexual sadists have been known to kill, and the victims of their lust murders have often been women who were complete strangers to them. But in the case before us, I doubt if X is your killer. With Mrs. Y readily available, he has at hand all he needs to satisfy himself and would not, one imagines, seek a casual 'extra.' So, gentlemen, though our knowledge concerning these matters is still fragmentary, I would say, as definitely as I dare, that X would not likely to be guilty of the homicide of a stranger.'

'That's fair enough, and very clearly put, sir,' Hallam said. 'I'm extremely grateful for your help. I've no further questions. Have you, Sergeant?'

'I'm just curious on one point, sir. What about the women? Do they like this knocking-about?'

Myers smiled. 'I'm not committing myself to pronouncements on the subject of such mysterious creatures as women, Sergeant Spratt. But I will venture to say that your Mrs. Y, obviously a spoiled creature, having had all her own way since she was a child, might find the caveman type refreshing as a novelty. She might even enjoy her experiences with him sexually, too.'

'D'you think all that puts Pettifer in the clear, sir?' Spratt asked when they were seated again in Hallam's office.

'We never could find a motive for him with regard to Madge Adkin, Jack. And now I'm sure his 'confession' in the taxi referred to Dora North.'

'True . . . I wish we knew why Madge noted Kaye's place twice in her diary, when, according to him, she couldn't possibly have made an unlawful entry. I wish we could have found one object in that collection of hers to prove she had got in, despite all appearances to the contrary.' He got up. 'That reminds me. I set Norwood and Packer and young Garrett to check the odd-number houses in Granville Road. Their reports should be in now.'

He went out to the main office and returned with the reports in his hand. 'They're back. I've told them they'd better hang on till we've looked through this lot.'

He squared up the papers on his desk, started to read. He put the first report aside after a moment, read the second carefully twice, glanced quickly through the third.

'There's a bit of a possibility here, sir,' he said. 'This could be quite helpful. And there was a message from Newton the estate agent, at the desk. He wants to see you urgently.'

21

'Packer and Norwood were dead unlucky,' Spratt said, flicking the reports before him, 'but Garrett, who seems fated to keep turning up in this case, got a nibble. From a Mrs. Dalby, at Number Twenty-five. 'When asked if she had ever seen anybody moving about late at night,'' Spratt read, ''she replied only that red-haired man who lives at Kayes. He often comes out of the kitchen door late on and goes into the storeplace they have under the house. As if he keeps fetching something from there but I've never been able to see what it was.''

Hallam's eyes sparked with interest. 'So, despite Kaye's careful locking up before he went to bed, the kitchen door was open for a short period some nights. We might have thought of that possibility.'

'What we did think, sir, was that when Kaye had gone to bed, his wife and lover-boy got down to it, all nice and cosy, and stayed that way.'

'Well, we'll follow it up. What's this about Newton?'

'Wants to see you — matter of some importance — would prefer you to go to his office but is willing to come here if that's more convenient.'

'Right. We'll go and see him first, then.'

Newton was all genial smile and outstretched hand. He settled them in chairs, pushed a cigarette box across his desk and said, 'Of course — not while on duty — I quite understand,' when they declined.

'Now, Chief Inspector — Sergeant — I know you are busy men. I'll make it as short as I can. I'm being black-mailed, or, to be more precise, an attempt at blackmail has been made, and in such matters I believe in informing the police at once.'

Hallam nodded. 'Always a wise proceeding, sir.'

'You will recollect that the last time you were here you questioned me as to my presence, on Friday afternoon, on Granville Common. A certain lady was also involved.

The blackmail attempt is connected with that meeting.'

'You mean West and the photograph he took, sir? But he assured me — '

'West? Oh, no, no, no! That's all cleared up. He came across to my house and apologized. No, this is a much dirtier business.'

The smile had gone from his face now. His mouth was drawn down, his eyes half shut. He sighed deeply.

'I'm afraid the sordid little story I have to tell you, gentlemen, is all too common.

'When the Kayes of Granville Road came to live in Deniston, they engaged this firm to find them a house. By chance we had the agency of a vacant residence in Granville Road and were able to negotiate a sale to Reginald Kaye. There were, however, some preliminary snags to iron out, with consequent delay before the conveyance was completed. During that time I saw a good deal of Mrs. Kaye, who came to the office here practically every day — they were staying at a hotel then — and always demanded to see me.

'Well . . . ' He shrugged his shoulders.

'Stella Kaye is an attractive woman. I took her out to lunch several times and then, quite suddenly, I became aware of the fact that if I cared to be more than just a friend to her, she would put no obstacles in my way. I was tempted. I fell. Of course, I should have had more sense.

'The affair, such as it was, did not last long. We began to quarrel mildly with each other — she was far too demanding — and then the rows became worse and she threatened to break it off. I fancy she had another man in view by then, and I'm pretty sure I could name him, but there's no need for that. I admit my masculine pride was hurt for, though I was tired of her by then, I would have preferred the break to have come from me and not from her. But taking it all round, I realized I was well out of it.

'I had been foolish enough to write her a number of quite — er — passionate letters, in reply to even more passionate ones she had written to me. We exchanged these, over a period of some weeks, whenever we met. I destroyed hers as soon as I had read them, and assumed she had done the same to mine. Instead, she kept them.

'I learnt this last Friday, at our meeting on the Common. She had made the appointment to see me there to tell me that the letters, some dozen of them, had disappeared from the place where she had put them. They were in a locked cedarwood box at the back of one of the dressing-table drawers in her bedroom. The box, and its contents, had disappeared.

'She couldn't account for this. Nobody, as far as she knew, was even aware of the box's existence. She had bought it without telling anyone of the purchase.'

'Does she employ domestic help, do you know, sir?'

'No. She never has done. She asked her two boys if they had seen the box, they denied any knowledge of it.'

'The husband? The guest?'

'Yes, I put those questions, too. She was certain that Mr. Whatever-his-name-is could not have taken it and she couldn't imagine her husband doing so. A complete mystery, she claimed.'

'What about the box key?'

'She still had it. She showed it me, on a ring with several others which she always keeps in her handbag. Actually, Chief Inspector, I was puzzled as to why she had made an appointment to tell me all this, but before I could mention this, that ass West appeared and stopped the discussion most effectively.

'Naturally, I have been rather worried since but I put the matter out of my mind as much as possible until last night, when a man telephoned me at my house. He said he had the letters I had written to Stella Kaye and would sell me the lot for £500 cash. He also said I would receive instructions later as to where to leave the money and collect the letters. He then rang off.'

Spratt had his notebook out.

'Can you describe the voice, sir?'

'The man spoke with a local accent. He was using a private telephone, not a call box. Apart from that, I can tell you nothing.

'Just one other point, though. When that foolish escapade of mine with Mrs.

Kaye was over, I had the sense to tell my wife all about it, and she forgave me when I asked her to. So the letters are of no value from the point of view of concealing the matter from her. They could damage my future career as a local councillor, though. However, I am quite prepared to give all thought of that up, if it means I have to pay blackmail money to hide an affair which could wreck that career. I shall not pay a penny.'

'That's the spirit, sir. When you hear from this man again, if you do, let us know at once. If you could keep him talking while somebody else rings us on another phone and tells us what is happening, we may catch him that way. His first call was designed to soften you up. If he rings again it will be soon, for he'll imagine he's got you in a fair state of stew by now. One last thing. You feel sure it was a man and not a woman imitating a man's voice?'

'As far as I can judge it was a man, Chief Inspector.'

'It must have been Kaye himself who whipped those letters if it wasn't Pettifer,'

Spratt commented as they drove towards Ashwood after a quick lunch. 'You know, Kaye is keeping Pettifer, when all's said and done. The bloke's practically given up his so-called practice, and he'll not have any capital to draw on. I'll bet Kaye even pays for his drinks and his fags — or Mrs. Kaye does, which comes to the same thing.'

'You mean, Kaye found those letters and saw a chance of screwing some money out of Newton? Hardly in character, is it?'

'He might be pushed pretty hard just now, sir. With a couple of kids, and a wife who throws it about plenty, and now lover-boy as well, it could be Kaye has begun to feel a pinch.'

'He's a bigger fool than I take him for if he's trying that game on with Newton,' Hallam grunted. 'No, I'm not betting on Kaye. There was — ' He broke off, and Spratt, glancing sideways, saw his chief was wrestling with a newly-born idea. 'I wonder how well-off Madge Adkin was,' Hallam said softly at last.

'I see. If Madge had managed to get

into Kaye's house, and had done a search and found those letters, and now somebody else has them, somebody who . . . But she took only small, worthless trophies, sir.'

'As far as we know,' Hallam reminded him, and Spratt muttered that, for his money, there were too many damn letters in this Adkin case.

Mrs. Bessie Dalby, of Granville Road, was a plump and faded blonde who, at fifty, had mistakenly believed a bright copper hair dye could do things for her. When Hallam told her their errand, she led them into the spotless lounge of the semi-detached house.

'So you've come about what I told that young man who was round this morning,' she said. 'D'you know, when he had gone I wished I'd never said anything. I did, really. I mean, I'm not the sort who pries and spies on my neighbours, and I wouldn't like people around here to think I did. But there again, we all have to help the police if we can, haven't we?'

'The point is, Mrs. Dalby,' Hallam

explained, 'we're looking into every hole and corner for an explanation of Miss Adkin's death. She was, as you know, found in a garden across the way. Nobody saw her killer, because nobody was out and about at the time of her death. Now you say you have seen the gentleman who lives opposite, Mr. Pettifer, come out of the house late at night sometimes.'

'Gentleman! Huh!' Mrs. Dalby pulled a face. 'I wouldn't call him that. Nor her opposite a lady, either. What the husband's thinking of to allow it, and with two little boys, too!' She was bubbling with indignation now. 'Oh, I could tell you plenty if I wanted!'

'I'm sure you could,' Hallam said soothingly, 'but what we're interested in is Mr. Pettifer coming out of the house late at night. If he did so on the night of Miss Adkin's death, he may have seen or heard something which could help us.'

'Why don't you ask him if he was outside that night, then?'

'Because he says he wasn't. Now, he may have genuinely forgotten what he actually did, but if you had seen him

— well, I could press his memory a bit, couldn't I?'

As an explanation it was weak enough, but it got by the copper-haired lady.

'Well, he was, and on that night, too, and I'm definitely certain about that because of my sleeping tablets.'

'Your sleeping tablets,' Hallam repeated gravely.

'Yes. I'm a poor sleeper and the doctor gives me tablets for it. Only I don't want to get to the stage where I have to rely on them to send me off. So I ration myself. I mean, I never take them before two o'clock in the morning. And several times, when I've got up to take the tablets, which means going to the bathroom for a drink of water, I've looked out of the bedroom window, like anybody would do, and I've seen that man come out of the kitchen door, at the side of the house. I saw him the night Miss Adkin was killed, because I couldn't get off to sleep then. It was the usual routine. He came out with a torch, went along to what was made for a coalshed under the side of the house, only it's a very big extensive place and they use it as a sort of store and keep the coals in big metal bins opposite the kitchen door. He unlocked the storeplace door, went in, came out with something in his hand. I couldn't swear to it but I think it was a bottle. I've seen him do that twice in a night, as if he was fetching something and then taking it back.'

'How long between the two journeys, Mrs. Dalby?'

'Oh, twenty minutes, half an hour, something like that.'

'And you're sure he was out early last Tuesday morning?'

'Positive. I can swear to that.'

'Thank you very much, Mrs. Dalby.' Hallam signed to Spratt, they both rose. 'We'll try to jog Mr. Pettifer's memory again. In fact, we'll go across there now and hope to find him in.'

'Oh, he's in all right — with her as usual.' Mrs. Dalby sniffed. 'You may find yourselves interrupting something, though. Don't be surprised at anything you see there.'

Hallam smiled. 'It takes a deal to

surprise a policeman,' he replied, and wished her good-day.

Spratt's ring at the Kayes' house was not answered immediately. He was about to press the bell a second time when the door opened. Mrs. Kaye stood there, blinking her large blue eyes and quite clearly suppressing a yawn. She wore her low-necked housecoat and her feet were shoeless. The housecoat had been buttoned carelessly and showed the top of a frilly black bra.

'Oh!' she said. 'It's you lot again. I was just having a nap on the settee. Can't you ever leave a girl in peace?'

'I'm sorry we have to be such a nuisance,' Hallam said quietly. 'Sorry, too, that you have been disturbed. But we have to talk to you. May we come in?'

She sighed exaggeratedly and stood aside. 'I suppose so. Go into the lounge, will you, while I slip upstairs and put a dress on. Your Sergeant Whatshisname obviously disapproves of me as I am.'

Spratt coughed shortly but, without reply, he followed his chief along the hall and into the lounge. The settee cushions were crumpled and awry and a pair of black shoes had been kicked off on the hearthrug. Hallam felt behind the cushions, but the cane had gone.

Stella Kaye did not keep them waiting long, though she had tidied her hair and freshened her make-up in addition to donning a dark green dress. She seemed to have recovered her former flirtatiousness and after inviting them to find chairs she put on her shoes, plumped up the settee cushions and sat down there, clasping her hands behind her head and looking provocatively from one to the other.

'Is Mr. Pettifer at home?' Hallam began.

'He's upstairs, also taking a nap, Chief. We had another of our late treatment sessions last night, and it seems I rather tired him out.' She giggled again. 'But don't say you want to see him. He's always in a hell of a bad mood when he first wakes up.'

'In that case, Mrs. Kaye, you can probably answer the questions I have to put. On the night Miss Adkin was killed, did Mr. Pettifer, after your husband had locked up and gone to bed, make one of his trips to your storeplace, by way of the kitchen door?'

Her hands came down to her sides. She sat forward.

'What do you mean, one of his trips?'

'Don't let's waste time, Mrs. Kaye. You know what I'm talking about. The point is, did he go out that night?'

She shrugged. 'You seem to know all about it. He may have done. I can't remember.'

'We have a witness who says he did. I want to check that with Mr. Pettifer.'

'Whatever for? I mean, even if he did go out to the store, what's the point? He saw nothing, heard nothing. We've already told you that.'

'As you don't remember about last Tuesday, I shall have to see him personally. Would you be good enough to ask him to come down here now?'

'Look, let's say he did. Well, he left me here, went out to the store to get something from it, brought it back into the lounge. That was all.'

'What was it he went for, Mrs. Kaye?'

'That's no business of yours.'

Hallam nodded cheerfully. 'Perhaps you're right. But you're going to be asked that question in Court, you know. Now, did he take this something back to the store later on?'

'As a matter of fact, he did.'

'And, during the time this something was in the house, was the kitchen door left unlocked?'

'Well, he wouldn't bother to lock it, would he, when he knew he was going out again in a short time? He locked it when he came back then. But what on earth has all this to do with Miss Adkin?'

'I'll come to that later. At the moment, I want to get a clear, detailed picture. Mr. Pettifer went into the kitchen from the lounge here, unlocked the outer door, went to the store, unlocked that door, brought a bottle back to the lounge, you had drinks, he took it back, and returned after locking both doors again. That is correct?'

'My God!' She spoke in a whisper. 'So somebody's been spying on us.' Her voice rose shrilly. 'Who is it? I've a right to know!'

'Take it easy, Mrs. Kaye,' Hallam warned. 'You must realize, in a case of this sort, where the possibility of a homicidal maniac hanging about the district cannot be ignored, the police must maintain a close watch in case the said maniac strikes again. We get about after dark, you know, and we keep our eyes open. But it's no concern of ours if you and your friend decide to have a drink before retiring. What I need to know is how long, approximately, that door could have been left open.'

'Ten minutes, maybe a quarter of an hour.'

'Could it have been half an hour?'

'Oh, I suppose so. But look here, Chief' — the honeyed tone and manner were back again now — 'you won't reveal our little secret, will you? You see, Sid likes a nightcap — whisky usually — and he's got me into the habit, too. But my husband is a bit stuffy on things like that. He won't have drink in the house. So Sid and I keep our drop of wallop in the store, which is full of household stuff — you know, tinned things and so on — and the door is always locked and I have the key. Neither my husband nor the boys ever go in there. So be a sport and keep it under your lid, won't you, dear?'

'We won't divulge anything unless it becomes absolutely necessary. Have you any questions, Sergeant?'

'I don't think so, sir.'

'In that case we'll be going.' He saw the look of relief which flickered in the woman's eyes. 'I hope we shan't have to trouble you again, Mrs. Kaye.'

Spratt chuckled as he slid behind the wheel of the car.

'"The police must maintain a close watch,"' he quoted. 'Nicely put, sir. Very nicely put indeed!'

22

The following morning, which was a Tuesday, a week after Madge Adkin's death, Charles Newton came downstairs all ready for the office. The telephone in the hall rang as he passed it. He picked it up.

'Would that be Mr. Newton?' a voice asked.

Newton covered the mouthpiece with his hand. 'Margaret!' he shouted. 'Margaret — here, quick!' But there was no reply to his summons. He swore, recollecting that his wife, a keen gardener, had said she must open the greenhouse ventilators first thing that morning. And, once get Margaret in her beloved greenhouse, and you had her there for at least an hour.

He put the receiver to his ear again.

'You there?' He caught a faint note of anxiety now in his caller's tone.

'Yes, this is Charles Newton speaking. I recognized your voice, I wanted to make sure my wife wasn't around. What is it?'

'You know. Got the money ready?'

'Yes, but look here. Even if I pay you what you demand, what guarantee have I you'll hand those letters over?'

'You'll get 'em. You've got to have 'em, haven't you?'

'You know that. But five hundred is a lot of money. Couldn't we agree on less?'

'I'm not bargaining, mate. Put the money in a brown paper parcel and, at dusk tonight, put the parcel in the ditch that runs down the side of Gypsy Lane. The far end, nearest the Common. And no funny business with the police, neither. I'll be watching.'

The phone went dead. Newton glanced at his watch and dialled Police Headquarters. He was put through to Hallam at the moment when, in his office, the Chief Inspector was hanging up his hat and coat.

Hallam listened carefully as Newton repeated the conversation he had just had. 'Very good, sir,' he said. 'No, don't apologize because you couldn't let us know he was ringing you. Put something

— papers, anything — in a parcel and leave it where you were told to. Let's see — sunset is about seven o'clock now, Summer Time. Do the job at seven-thirty, will you? Good. We'll be covering our end of it. Just deposit the parcel and get out of there fast.'

He nodded good morning to Spratt as his sergeant came in. 'Make all the necessary arrangements, will you, Jack?' he said when he had given Spratt the gist of Newton's report. 'I suggest you put Garrett on to the Gypsy Lane end. He seems to know how to keep hidden. I want to go over to Kaye's office this morning.'

Spratt nodded and went out to the main C.I.D. office. Garrett, still seconded to the department, had been put that morning on to the job of file-checking and indexing. Spratt called the young constable over.

'I've a job for you this evening. Here's the set-up.'

Garrett listened attentively. When Spratt ended with, 'Well, can you do it?' he nodded thoughtfully.

'I think so, Sarge. There's not much ground cover in Ash Wood at that end, and I'll have to be somewhere handy if I'm going to spot this joker. A tree sounds the best bet. I'd slip in off Ashwood Road, beyond Crane's place. I could get along the far side of the hedge between his two fields without being seen. That'd land me in Ash Wood, and I could make my way towards the end of Gypsy Lane without any trouble.'

'Maybe you'd better go up there and have a recce first.'

'Doesn't matter, Sarge. I know my way about well enough, and maybe, if I went there earlier, I might be seen. I'll be okay.' He hesitated, and then, 'What about the Cranes, Sarge? Are they going to cop out for sheltering Fred Mitchell? I mean, have you got him definitely clear of Madge Adkin's killing?'

'I'd be surprised if he did it, lad. As for the Cranes, I'm not speaking officially, but I don't reckon they'll be in much trouble. Yes, Birch?'

'Young woman outside, Sarge. Wants to see you. Name of Dora North.'

'Show her into Mr. Hallam's room. I'll see her there.' He turned to Garrett again. 'Carry on with this job and see me later — we'll say four o'clock this afternoon — for a last check-up on tonight's job.'

Dora North was already seated comfortably in the visitor's chair when Spratt walked into the Chief Inspector's room. Dora looked radiant. Her blue-black hair, newly set, her deep brown eyes and warmly-coloured cheeks all seemed to glow and sparkle.

'Hullo, Mr. Spratt!' She smiled at him. 'Have you found out who wrote me those anonymous letters yet?'

'We're working on it, Dora.'

She waved her hands expansively. 'Don't waste your time.'

'You mean you know where they came from?'

'I haven't the faintest idea. And I don't care — that!' She snapped her fingers. 'Not now, I don't.'

Spratt regarded her carefully, gravely.

'You're all in the clouds this morning, aren't you, young lady? You hopped up with purple hearts or something?'

'No. I'm just feeling — ooh, right marvellous.' Her perfect teeth flashed at him. 'I feel so good I could jump up, throw my arms round your neck and give you a big loving kiss.'

'So somebody has left you a fortune, then.'

' 'Tisn't that, either, though I did get a big kick when I got to work yesterday morning. I'm being transferred to our posh branch in Globe Street as from next week. It's a promotion and I've a chance to work up to manageress.'

She clasped her hands on her lap and became serious.

'No. What I'm feeling so good about is something else, Mr. Spratt. You see — it's hard to put just right — but, well, it's like as if I've been in prison, loaded down with chains and now I'm out again and free. It's smashing.'

'What you're trying to say — let me guess — is you don't care the toss of a brass button for Sid Pettifer any more.'

'You've hit it in one. Look, Mr. Spratt, I got to know Sid, and he started feeding me this line about him being a wonderful healer with a gift the world wouldn't recognize and that touched me on my soft side and I felt sorry for him. Well, he took me out once or twice and then I began to go across to his room in Dean Street. I was more interested in him than sorry for him by then. You see, he was so different, like, from all the other fellows I'd ever been out with.' She moved restlessly. 'Look, I'm taking up your time, and you don't want to listen, anyway.'

'You're wrong there, Dora. Just you carry on. How was he different?'

'Well, he didn't seem keen on petting, like. I mean, not wanting to kiss me and that. I thought I must be losing my sex-appeal. Because he didn't strike me as a shy type.

'So one night, when we were at the pictures, I thought I'd better make a move and I held his hand. Cor! I soon wished I hadn't had that idea . . . He just got hold of my fingers with his and I might have had them in a screwed-up vice. I whispered to him he was hurting me, but it was like he didn't hear me. He sat there staring at the screen and squeezing my fingers till I nearly screamed. I kicked him hard on the ankle and then he did let go.

'When we came out, I told him how much he'd hurt me and he said he was sorry. But that was the start, like. Afterwards, when we were alone, he'd always want to be smacking and pummelling me, he did it like it was a joke, but when he really got going he didn't seem able to stop.'

'Funny sort of love-making, Dora. But maybe you got a thrill out of it?'

'Not me. But I had fallen for the chap and I couldn't stop myself seeing him. Then she came along — you know — and set herself to take him from me.

'Like a fool, I tried to fight back. I hadn't a chance against all she offered to do for him. I even went up to her house once or twice and tried to get him back. I'd lost my head over him, that's what. And I went through hell with myself.

'Then, last Sunday morning — you know — when you came to our place and she barged in with him, well, it was like that fellow in the Bible when the scales fell from his eyes. I looked at Sid, and then I looked at you and at our Dan, and I thought, Why'm I all steamed up about a queer like him, when there's so many nice guys in the world? And that was that, as far as I was concerned. I'm free of him now, and glad of it. I told Dan and he said I should come and see you because of the letters.'

'I'm pleased you did, Dora, and I'm glad you aren't worrying about Pettifer any more, too. You're far too nice a girl for him . . . What about that row you had in his room, you screaming and so on? Mr. Walsh, the printer on the floor below, was worried when he heard you.'

'Yes. We had a real set-to. Over her, of course. I smacked his face and he got hold of me round the neck — ' She stopped. 'You're thinking about that Miss Adkin, aren't you? But I still say Sid didn't do that. When he half-strangled me it was because he'd lost his temper, because I made him mad. I mean, it was different from how he'd handled me before. Like as if his queer part had gone and he was doing what any man would who'd blown his top. And unless that Miss Adkin had rowed with him, for quite a time, he'd never have . . . And why should she row with him at all?' She glanced at the wall clock. 'I'll have to be going, Mr. Spratt, only I'm on late turn this morning and Dan said I should drop in here first.'

Spratt got to his feet. 'Just one thing. You said you couldn't offer Pettifer what Mrs. Kaye could. Meaning?'

'Well, a posh home, a car, money, of course.'

'She gave him money? More than his treatment fees?'

'Yes. He shot off his mouth a lot about it. Ten quid, twenty, twenty-five — wads like that. He said he'd only got to put on a moan about being skint and next day she'd be pressing it into his hand.'

Spratt sniffed. 'Must have a very generous husband, unless she has money of her own.'

'I wouldn't know about that.' She smiled her thanks as Spratt opened the door for her and when he wished her good luck with the new job she winked saucily at him.

'Lots of nice boys use our Globe Street place. Wow! I just can't wait! Come in and see me operating sometime!'

23

Hallam walked thoughtfully towards Bellman Street, where the offices of Sims and Forrester, Kaye's employers, were situated. He was on a ticklish mission and he realized he would need all his tact, and a slice of good luck as well, to bring it to a successful conclusion.

He got his slice of good luck. As he turned into Bellman Street he saw Reginald Kaye hurrying towards him. Kaye pulled up as he recognized Hallam.

'Good morning, Chief Inspector! Anything new?'

Hallam put on a rueful grin and shook his head.

'Not yet, I'm afraid. We have some hopes, but that's all at the moment.'

Kaye said, 'I must be getting along. I'm on an out-of-town job, I'm just going to get my car from where I parked it.'

'Big job, sir?'

Kaye shrugged. 'I'll be lucky if I finish

it today. Good morning, Chief Inspector.'

Hallam returned the compliment and strode on, jubilant now. The one thing he wanted was to have Reginald Kaye kept out of his hair this morning. He wasn't usually superstitious, but, as he'd noticed before, getting a piece of good fortune in a case was always significant. It meant things were moving towards a break, nine times out of ten.

He entered a handsome office building with 'Sims & Forrester, Chartered Accountants' lettered in gold across the ground floor windows. At an inquiry desk, a smart young woman seemed doubtful as to whether he could see Mr. Forrester without an appointment. Mr. Sims, she explained, was no longer with them. Hallam gathered the implication and nodded with due solemnity. The woman said if he would wait she would go and see and Hallam gave her one of his official cards to make her investigations easier.

She returned, all smiles, to say Mr. Forrester would be delighted if the Chief Inspector would come along at once. Hallam was shown upstairs into an imposing modern office overlooking the street. Forrester was an elderly man with thick-rimmed spectacles, a keen face and a mouth which suggested that any balance sheet which did not show perfect equilibrium, even to the extent of a halfpenny, had better look out for itself. He rose from behind his desk and shook hands.

'A visit from the police is a unique occasion here, Chief Inspector,' he said. 'My curiosity is indeed aroused. I trust nothing is wrong in any way?'

'I'm looking into a small matter of some anonymous letters, sir. These are harmless enough in themselves, being neither libellous nor obscene. But they form part of a more important case, and I wish to trace the writer. They — I have two of them — are typewritten. I have some reason to think they were produced in this office.'

'Good God!' Forrester, who had remained standing, now sank hurriedly into his chair. 'You don't say so!'

'Of course, I may be completely mistaken, sir.'

'But you have to make sure. I know. Sit down, and we will get my personal secretary on to this. Secretary!' He grinned as he pressed a key on his desk inter-com. 'Mrs. Cox practically runs this place!'

Mrs. Cox, who came briskly into the room, was a handsome, grey-haired woman, extremely smartly dressed, with the competent, assured air of a casualty ward sister prepared to deal with anything from a scratched finger to a severed artery. When her employer had explained the reason for Hallam's visit, she held out a beautifully-manicured hand.

'May I see the documents in question, if you please?'

Hallam took out the two letters Dora North had given to Spratt and handed them across the desk. Mrs. Cox removed the letters in turn from their envelopes, glanced at the typewritten lines and held both sheets, and the envelopes, up to the light.

'Cheap brand these.' She threw the envelopes down. 'Get them at any small shop. We don't use stuff like that here.

But the letter paper is quite a good bond. We have some of this particular brand in stock, but so have scores of other offices in Deniston, I'm willing to bet. The typing looks as if it may have been done on a portable rather than on a standard machine!' She put the letters on the desk by the envelopes. 'Give me ten minutes, and I'll have a specimen from every machine in this office.'

'Which makes everything most convenient,' Forrester said as the admirable Mrs. Cox hurried out. 'It is coffee time, and you will do me the honour of joining me, Chief Inspector? Good.' He spoke into his inter-com and coffee in delicate cups on a silver tray was there almost at once. It was clear that Sims and Forrester were well-organized.

No further reference was made to Hallam's visit while they drank. They discussed a recent case of fraud which the local C.I.D. had successfully investigated and Forrester, sipping his coffee, was duly complimentary. Hallam relaxed with a pipe, enjoyed the excellent brew and was not impatient when Mrs. Cox's ten minutes became twenty.

'Some of these girls!' she said when she came in. 'Can't take a simple instruction, must know why, must be told exactly what to type as a specimen. Here you are — from eighteen machines, including my own.'

Hallam laid his pipe aside. It was not long before he glanced up, with a shake of his head, at the two who were watching him intently.

'Nothing here, I'm afraid. Both the letters were done on the same machine — that's obvious. You suggested a portable, Mrs. Cox. How many of those have you in the office?'

'My own and Mr. Bodilam's — he's the junior partner. These are they.' She indicated two of the specimens.

Hallam examined them again. 'No, they don't fit. Forgive the question, Mrs. Cox, but are there definitely no more typewriters in the office?'

Mrs. Cox was not affronted. 'I could swear there aren't, but I'll check the stock book.' She left them again and Hallam pushed the letters, and the specimens of typing, across the desk.

'Will you have a look at these, sir? I'd like a second opinion.' It was one of his rules that a little flattery never did harm.

Forrester had not examined more than seven of the specimens, shaking his head gravely as he put each aside, when Mrs. Cox arrived for the third time, carrying a large, leather-bound book.

'I'd forgotten the old Juventa!' she exclaimed. 'It was an out-of-date portable we'd had for decades and the platen had gone completely. We wrote it off, but Mr. Kaye saw it lying around and said he'd take charge of it. He thought he could repair it and have a new platen fixed. He likes mechanical problems, says it's a change from figures.'

'Would it be possible for me to see Mr. Kaye?'

Forrester shook his head. 'I'm sorry, but he's out of town today. However, I've no doubt Mrs. Cox will take a look round his office for us. He won't mind, we have nothing to hide in this firm.'

'Shuttle service,' Mrs. Cox remarked from the door. 'But no doubt it's good for my figure.'

Perturbed now, Forrester looked anxiously at Hallam.

'You surely don't connect Kaye with these letters, Chief Inspector? Look at the mis-spellings, the lack of punctuation. Kaye is an educated man.'

'Possible red herrings, sir. In any case, I must ask for your utmost silence regarding my visit here this morning. Mrs. Cox's, too.'

'Of course! Of course! That goes without saying.' But Forrester was upset now. He couldn't find anything to utter but broken, never-finished sentences. His speechlessness was complete when Mrs. Cox returnd with a battered, Italian-made portable, set it on the desk and, having typed half-a-dozen lines on a sheet of paper, pulled it out and gave it to Hallam. After a brief glance he beckoned her to his side.

'No doubt at all,' she said when she had made a comparison. 'I found this machine in the bottom drawer of his desk. For good measure, here's the rest of the packet of envelopes which match these two. They were in the drawer under the typewriter.'

24

Dusk was approaching when Garrett got off the bus at the Ashwood terminus. He walked towards Gypsy Lane, thinking over the brief conference which had been held in Hallam's office that afternoon. Detective Constable Norwood had been there with the Chief Inspector and Sergeant Spratt. The two younger men had been given their orders and Hallam had closed the meeting by saying, 'If we all do our jobs well tonight, with a bit of luck we'll clear up this case.' Back on patrol tomorrow, then, Garrett thought. Well, it had been a nice break.

He passed the end of Gypsy Lane and walked along by the edge of the field in which Crane's house and buildings stood. There was nobody about, and, having made doubly sure he was not observed, Garrett slipped over a fenced gap and began to make his way along the far side of the hedge. A barbed wire fence, where the hedge ended, cut the field off from Ash Wood. Garrett negotiated this carefully.

Despite its name, ashes were sparsely scattered in the wood. There was an abundance of oaks, a few scrubby birches and here and there a tall sycamore. Keeping well clear of James Tanner's bungalow and cultivated ground, Garrett moved quietly towards the corner of the wood near the lower end of Gypsy Lane. It was still light enough for country-bred vision, and to his satisfaction he found an oak tree placed perfectly for him. He sprang from the ground to hook his fingers on to a lateral branch stout enough to take his weight. A heave and a squirming push and he was up. He settled into a comfortable fork and looked about him.

He could see the line of the ditch between the lane and the wood. He had an excellent view of the rear premises of the lowest houses on that side of Granville Road — the Kayes' detached house and the Rennisons' and Bentons' semis. There were lights in the lower rooms of all three houses. A blurred movement caught his eye — a first-floor window pushed open at the Kayes'. Somebody — he couldn't distinguish who — leaned out and stayed in that position for almost five minutes. There was no sign of Newton, but according to plan he would already have deposited his parcel in the ditch, approaching it from the Common end.

There came the sound of the window closing quietly. Almost at once one of the french doors of Number Twenty-six was opened, the light above it which illuminated the terrace came on. Garrett heard Pettifer's voice.

'Nah, then, you two. A bit o' floodlit football afore you goes to bed, eh?' He ran down the terrace steps on to the lawn, bouncing a large white rubber ball and followed by the two young Kayes. Garrett saw their mother appear, to lean against the doorway, watching them.

With a good deal of shouting and mock enthusiasm from Pettifer, a ragged sort of game began. It continued for some minutes until Pettifer, with a great lunge, booted the ball over the garden fence into Gypsy Lane.

'And that will be that,' Stella Kaye called. 'Come on in, boys. Uncle Sid will go and fetch the ball.'

Garrett grinned to himself as Pettifer came round into the lane from the front of the house, making a great search for a ball which lay in plain view on the edge of the lane. He was darting anxious glances around him as he ranged about, gradually getting nearer to the end of the ditch. Then, with a quick movement he stooped, lifted a brown paper-covered packet from the ditch, picked up the ball and hurried off round the corner of the house.

Garrett dropped to earth. He glanced at his watch. It was quite dark when, a quarter of an hour later, he pushed away from the tree against which he had been leaning and made his way to the Common end of Granville Road. He greeted a tall figure which moved out of the shadows.

'Okay, Barry?'

'Went just like Hallam said it would,' Norwood replied. 'He and Jack Spratt should be along any minute now. I reckon Kaye hasn't got home yet, the garage is still empty. Here they are.'

Hallam and Spratt appeared from the drive gates of Number Eleven. They crossed the road, joined the two constables and received their reports.

'You two can go off now,' Hallam said. 'Get all that written down and typed and bring it to me in the morning. You've both done well. Good night.'

Spratt rang the bell at the Kayes' house. It was answered by Pettifer.

'Thought you lot had finished here,' he said surlily. 'I don't see as how we can — Hey, do you mind?' But the detectives did not bother to apologize as they pushed past him into the house.

'Mr. Kaye is not back yet?' Pettifer shook his head and Hallam went on, 'Where is Mrs. Kaye?'

'Upstairs. Putting the kids to bed.'

'Right. Go and ask her to come down as soon as possible, Sergeant. Pettifer, you and I will go into the lounge.'

'We'll 'ell as like. You can't come here ordering me about!'

'It's either here or at the station. Please yourself.' Pettifer's shoulders moved angrily but he led the way into the lounge. 'When is Mr. Kaye expected back?'

'Should be here any time now. He rang up, said he'd be home later'n usual.'

Hallam nodded. He could hear Stella Kaye coming downstairs, protesting to Spratt in a high, querulous voice. She came into the lounge like a wild cat. Hallam put up a hand.

'All right, all right! Save your breath. You two are in a mess, and you can't talk yourselves out of it. Blackmail is an ugly crime, and if I had my way I'd be charging both of you with it. As it is, you're lucky. Your intended victim refuses to press charges, but only on account of those two youngsters upstairs.'

'I don't know what on earth you're yammering about!' Stella Kaye said.

'Don't be stupid, Mrs. Kaye. You and Pettifer have been trying to extort money from Mr. Charles Newton. In itself, that is a criminal offence.'

'You've absolutely no proof of such an accusation!'

'I have a witness who saw Pettifer take the parcel which he had told Mr. Newton to leave in the Gypsy Lane ditch — '

'I found it by accident, when I were looking for a ball!'

'A ball which you deliberately kicked over into the lane, which lay in full view there and needed no looking for.'

'I tell you, I come across the parcel o' newspapers by accident — '

'And, having found it contained paper only, you were fool enough to ring Mr. Newton and threaten him with what you would do if he tricked you again. Sergeant Spratt and I were waiting at Mr. Newton's house for you to ring. We guessed you'd feel compelled to do this at once.'

'I never rang nobody tonight, did I, Stella?'

'I had a man waiting in Mr. Rennison's garden. When the light went on for you to use the telephone in the hall here he slipped across the fence and listened outside the window where the instrument stands on the ledge. He saw you using it, I have a record of your conversation. So don't give me any more of your lip, or I'll run you in now!'

He swung round to Spratt.

'That sounds like the car arriving. Ask Mr. Kaye to join us, Sergeant.'

Kaye came in, pulling off his driving gloves, his face a mask of puzzlement.

'Hullo, Hallam! What goes on?'

'The end of a most unpleasant business, sir. I've a few things to say, you'd better all sit down and listen.' Standing on the hearth rug, he waited while Pettifer and Mrs. Kaye subdued now, took the settee. Kaye shrugged off his coat, let it fall to the floor. He sat in one of the easy chairs and Spratt leaned negligently against the door.

'You have a wife, Mr. Kaye,' Hallam said, 'who is, to use a North Country expression, man-fond.' His hand went up to quash Kaye's protest. 'You know this, I'm sure. She has tried her wiles on quite a few men in the past, often with a success which must have become boringly easy for her. Then she met Pettifer.

'She found him intriguingly different from the others, for where they had been adoring, gentlemanly, he was rough with her, for his own satisfaction, and nobody had ever tried to master her before. She had always been given in to. By you, Mr. Kaye, especially.

'She knew you wouldn't — shall I say dare? — to object to her bringing Pettifer into this house. For the sake of your boys you wanted no trouble. You probably thought she'd soon tire of Pettifer, as she had of the others. But it must have been bitterly galling to you.

'You were having to keep Pettifer, to pay for his food, his cigarettes, his drink, because your wife had insisted he gave up his Dean Street practice, to devote all his time to her. But you have heavy committments here — this house, the children's education, your wife's extravagant tastes. You wanted to get Pettifer out of here, to break up his friendship with your wife, and I think you saw, by using the can't-afford-it argument, a reasonable chance to do this. So you began to stick your toes in.'

He noted, by Kaye's shrug, that he had hit the mark.

'This was a cause for alarm to your wife and Pettifer. To get hold of some money of their own, to counter your arguments, they devised a scheme to blackmail a certain person whose letters Mrs. Kaye had. She told this person, as ground bait to the scheme, that she had lost them from a locked box in a private drawer. Very amateurish. And meanwhile, you, sir, were doing all you dare to rid your home of Pettifer.

'You wrote anonymously to Dora North, Pettifer's former girl friend, urging her to make a fight for him. You used the old Juventa portable at your office.'

Kaye's chin was sunk on his chest. He muttered words which Hallam only just managed to catch.

'A damned dirty trick to play. But I haven't been thinking clearly lately. And the taxi-driver. I sent him to report to you what Pettifer had said because I thought I saw a chance . . . '

'In the early hours of last Tuesday morning,' Hallam continued, 'you came downstairs. Your wife and your guest were still in this room. Probably, and quite naturally, you wanted to find out just what they were up to. You moved quietly along the hall and then you realized there was someone in the kitchen, just inside the back door, I imagine. And you attacked this person.'

Kaye's head jerked up. 'I thought it was Pettifer. I knew he was encouraging my wife to drink spirits. I saw a figure in trousers and something seemed to snap. Before I realized it was a woman's throat my fingers were gripping I'd gone too far. She was standing on the top step, I let her go and she fell, striking her head on the concrete. I swear it was a mistake! I've lived in hell ever since that moment. But there were the boys to consider . . . I couldn't own up to what I'd done.'

'Miss Adkin was on enclosed premises, at night,' Hallam said gently. 'That may help you. Go on, Mr. Kaye.'

'When I realized she was dead I carried her out on to the terrace. Stella and that fellow there had heard nothing, I knew. When they'd gone to bed, I carried her along the path, where I wouldn't leave traces, and put her in Rennison's garden. Then, in the morning, I pretended to discover her there, acting out the pretence in case I was being observed going down the garden, by any of the neighbours.'

He stood up. 'You are going to charge me, Chief Inspector. Will you grant me the favour of doing so at the police station, and not here? This was a happy home for me — once.'

And then he lunged forward, seized Pettifer by the front of his shirt and hauled him upright. Spratt stepped hastily in, but halted, well content, at Hallam's half-perceptible head-shake. Pettifer yelped in fear as Kaye's long right straightened him up. The piston-like left which took the healer on the chin sent him cartwheeling over the back of the settee. He jerked to stillness on the floor, whimpering.

Stella Kaye rushed forward and flung her arms round her husband.

'Reg! Reg, darling! I've been a fool — I didn't realize — '

Almost casually, but with some force, Kaye pushed her away from him. He glanced at the moaning Pettifer.

'I should have done that long ago,' he said with a grin of wry satisfaction. 'Well, Chief Inspector, shall we go?'

THE END

We do hope that you have enjoyed reading this large print book.

Did you know that all of our titles are available for purchase?

We publish a wide range of high quality large print books including:
Romances, Mysteries, Classics
General Fiction
Non Fiction and Westerns

Special interest titles available in large print are:
The Little Oxford Dictionary
Music Book, Song Book
Hymn Book, Service Book

Also available from us courtesy of Oxford University Press:
Young Readers' Dictionary
(large print edition)
Young Readers' Thesaurus
(large print edition)

For further information or a free brochure, please contact us at:

Ulverscroft Large Print Books Ltd.,
The Green, Bradgate Road, Anstey,
Leicester, LE7 7FU, England.
Tel: (00 44) **0116 236 4325**
Fax: (00 44) **0116 234 0205**

Other titles in the
Linford Mystery Library:

MURDER IN DUPLICATE

Peter Conway

When Jennifer Prentice, a student nurse, was found dead in a locked bathroom, Inspector Newton went to St. Aldhelm's Hospital to investigate . . . Newton finds the Matron, Miss Diana Digby Scott, unapproachable. Why was Alison Carter so disliked by Jennifer? Is Vernon Pritchard, the surgeon who was having an affair with Jennifer, telling the truth? Before Newton finds any answers, there is another death and he faces mortal danger himself.

A QUESTION OF MURDER

R. H. Lees

When Arthur Burnett died in the Rhodesian bush, Randall realised that Burnett was the one mentioned in the cryptogram. Inspector Sturman ridiculed Randall's suggestion that it could be foul play. So Randall proves that one of Burnett's African employees had been murdered and finds a mystic hill which only one African would dare to climb . . . Whilst observing animal behaviour, he comes upon a gruesome scene and almost loses his own life before solving the mystery.